Grozdana Lukic was born in Benkovac, a town in the Northern Dalmatia, in Croatia. In 1997, at the age of 21, she moved to Melbourne in Australia with her parents and two brothers, where she has lived since. Grozdana studied at the RMIT University in Melbourne and after completing the Degree in Social Science, she worked with newly arrived refugees and migrants assisting with their resettlement.

In 2017, Grozdana moved to another role where she is case managing complex offenders in the justice system.

Grozdana is supported by her loving husband, Lui, and is a proud mother of three wonderful children, son, Milan, and daughters, Leilani and Tina.

To all those who have embarked on a journey of self-discovery,
To the brave souls seeking their roots amidst the shadows of the past,
To those who have faced the pain of shattered memories,
And to the resilient hearts who dare to embrace the unknown.
This book is dedicated to you.
May Ornella's journey inspire and remind you that even in the darkest of times,
the strength to reclaim your true identity lies within.

Grozdana Lukic

Return into the Unknown

Austin Macauley Publishers™
London * Cambridge * New York * Sharjah

A CIP catalogue record for this title is available from the British Library.

ISBN 9781035817832 (Paperback)
ISBN 9781035817849 (ePub e-book)

www.austinmacauley.com

First Published 2023
Austin Macauley Publishers Ltd®
1 Canada Square
Canary Wharf
London
E14 5AA

Introduction

In December of 1995, after I turned 20, I wrote this novel. That was before I travelled to Australia in 1997 and started living here. At that time, I could only imagine and visualise in my mind a life far away from home. I never dreamt of actually having a chance to go to Australia and start a new chapter of my life. We often think there is no magic in this life, but just thinking of those few sentences above leads me to believe that magic is all around us because there is no other explanation that I can find to explain my unexpected arrival to this amazing land.

In 1995, my life hit rock bottom, having been a refugee in Serbia after my family fled the civil war in Croatia, barely escaping death. It was a dark age where the only way to escape reality was to live in your own imagination. It was the time when I gave up on my dreams to ever live the life, I prepared myself for during my childhood and early teenage years. It was a time where nothing really made sense and I had to distract myself to avoid thinking about my situation.

I had already given up and left University in February of 1995, accepting that I wasn't going to be an educated, free and independent woman. I was going to be a lawyer, but it was not meant to be. My dreams would turn into a nightmare from which I saw no escape. So, whilst I was writing this novel, when at work as a waitress serving the drunk and disillusioned youth of Serbia at the time, I was dreaming through the eyes of my heroine who was able to live a life I could not.

Prior to that, while working as a waitress near a soccer stadium in Belgrade, Serbia, I unexpectedly met someone who would inspire me to write this story. Although this story is fictional, it was inspired by the real events which occurred on the start of 4 August 1995, when the Croatian army launched a military offensive called Operation Storm, in which Croatian forces regained almost all the territory seized in 1991 by rebel Croatian Serbs.

Following the Operation Storm, hundreds of thousands of ethnic Serbs were expelled and left their ancestral homes, running away towards Bosnia and Serbia to save their lives. As Bosnia was still in the midst of its own civil war majority of these people ended up in Serbia as refugees. I was one of them. Having lost everything we had, my family, through some extended family connections, found a place in a village where five of us lived in one room until we figured out what to do next.

At 20 years old and full of life and energy, I personally found it very difficult to sit out and do nothing, so I went looking for work and eventually found a job in Belgrade where I was to work as a waitress every single day in a month for what is now equivalent to 100 Australian dollars. Not much could be bought for such a small amount of money but just the opportunity to be out and about was better than doing nothing.

One day whilst working in the restaurant I noticed a group of Roma kids who were coming in groups and begging. There was one thing unusual about the group this time as there with them was a small, blonde and skinny boy who was wearing an army looking jacket. Refugees would often be seen with such clothes as many came with only what they had on them at the time. This sight intrigued me, so I went out of the restaurant and called the boy in army jacket to come to me. He came immediately and introduced himself as Aleksandar.

I asked him where he was from and what he was doing out with the kids who were begging and he told me his life story in only a few sentences. He told me his father died in the war in Croatia and that he was an only child. At the time when I met him, he was 8 years old.

During Operation Storm, he and his mother were running away, however she was killed and he continued his escape with his paternal uncle. Once they reached the safety in Serbia, his uncle handed him over to an orphanage where he was now living with other orphans and abandoned or unwanted children. This story moved me deeply and I felt an instant connection to this poor soul.

Like myself, he was from Croatia, but unlike me, he had no family that wanted him. I asked him to come and visit me daily so that I could give him some food or part of my own tips. He did come almost every day and we became close friends.

One day, I asked him to come with me to the village where I was living with my family and he did. I offered him cooked food and spent time with him. He was quiet, looking sad. I thought he would be happy spending some time with a family who was from a familiar place as him, but it was not like that. He barely spoke and was distant and shy. On the bus, as we were returning back, he again seemed distant and did not speak. Although I was only 20 at the time, I could see there were deeper issues at hand and that he perhaps needed mental health support, but I was not able to do anything about it.

As time was passing, his presentation was changing and within a year of knowing him, I noticed that one day he was buying a packet of cigarettes. I asked him who the cigarettes were for and he told me they were for him. At this time, he was approximately 9 years old so I tried explaining to him that this was quite dangerous for his young lungs and that no good could come out of that. The change I noticed in him continued and he no longer was an easy-going chatty kid but distant and quieter as if removed from the reality.

I still kept looking for him and spending little time I could talking to him and advising him as something of an older sister, but he was not the same. As if his soul gave up and transformed into someone who had to grow up much sooner than his time. There was no shine in his eyes, only sadness and grief. He no longer wanted to speak of Croatia and his life with his parents. When asked if his uncle was visiting, he said his uncle's wife did not like him, so his uncle stopped visiting him. He was completely alone.

After this time, I did not see him anymore, although I looked for him in the usual places. One day, after at least, a couple of weeks since I saw him last, I approached the group of kids he used to hang around and asked about Aleksandar. One of the boys spoke to me and asked me if I did not know what happened. I confirmed that I knew nothing and curiously asked him to tell me what was going on.

This boy told me that approximately two weeks ago while they were walking around this area, a man approached them and asked Aleksandar who he was and why he was wearing the army jacket. Apparently, this man was someone who came from abroad but was originally from Croatia. Aleksandar told him about his life story and this man felt so sad for him and gave him 50 US dollars to buy something for himself.

As soon as this man left, the other boys, older than Aleksandar, asked him to hand the money over but he refused. These boys used wooden bats to beat him up in order to get the money from him and in the process fractured his skull and injured him badly. According to the boy telling me this story, Aleksandar was hospitalised and no one knew if he was going to survive.

Few weeks after, I managed to find a job closer to where I was living, so I had to leave the area without ever knowing what happened to Aleksandar or if he had survived. I was deeply hurt and angry after learning what happened to him. That poor orphan had no chance to make it in a cruel and selfish world. I would start to write this novel at my new job, where I was a waitress again, but in a small and quiet place.

Writing came easy for me and provided an escape from the world where I lived, the world where wars repeatedly occurred. I grew up reading and listening about World War 1 and 2. During my school years from grade 1 to grade 12, it was again all about the wars. When the war started during my teenage years, there was no surprise only sadness.

So, whilst I was writing this novel a strange coincidence occurred that I was not aware of until much later. My older brother had submitted an application for resettlement of our family as refugees with the United Nations High Commissioner of Refugees (UNHCR), begging for another chance in the developed world. My family by this time had lost everything. Our home was burned and possessions lost. But we were glad we escaped with our lives.

My older brother later told me he submitted that application in September of 1995 and he was told that if within three months the family was not contacted for an interview, he was to assume that application was rejected. It is strange how the laws of attractions were at play here. Only years later was I able to put things together and realise that perhaps there were 'invisible' laws at play, calming the chaos and pushing us forward on our path.

In early 1997, a call was received from the UNHCR inviting my father to attend an interview for the resettlement. The person who contacted was surprised that my family was still living in Serbia as refugees and within three months our application was approved.

However, at that stage, it was not clear where would our family settle. Is it going to be USA, Canada, New Zealand or who knows where? My father who was 47 years old at the time was not so excited, the thought of living in a foreign country where he was not able to communicate, being surrounded by unfamiliar faces. He felt the loss of his homeland strongly and grieved for the country whose tragic demise we all witnessed.

On the other hand, my brothers and I became quite excited and waited patiently for the next call which came as expected. We were to travel to Melbourne in Australia on permanent visas allowing us to live in Australia indefinitely. We were told within two years of staying in Australia we would be able to apply for citizenship. This news came as a shock to me as in my imagination I had already been living there through my fictional character from this novel. On 20 March 1997, my family and I landed at the Melbourne International Airport and the new chapter of my life started.

It was not easy as we had to let go and allow ourselves to live in peace once again but far from familiarity. When you settle in a foreign land, I feel those who meet us there think we came with empty bags and empty pages written in the book of our life. Instead, the bags may be empty, but our hearts are full and we bring with us our history and experiences.

In the foreign world, at the age of 21, I decided to push myself to my limits and go out there to claim my right to happiness and prosperity. As years were passing and I was making one after another milestone in my life the thought would cross my mind about my novel and if I should translate it into English and attempt having it published, but doubt would set in quickly and I would let the thought pass.

In September 2022 that thought came back again and I went looking for my handwritten manuscript which I put away somewhere hidden from eyes. I started reading it and by doing that I started connecting with myself 27 years ago when the novel was written. I thought if I do not translate it now, maybe I never will.

The war in my homeland finished in August 1995 but the pain still lived vividly in my mind. A life in my new motherland was just a blur in comparison to the strength of emotions and memories experienced while living there. And although the novel I wrote was a fiction, it felt real as I heard all sorts of stories over the years about what my people lived through.

This book is devoted to my beloved Yugoslavia, a country where I was born and the country I will be missing as long as I live. For many, just a name from history books, but for me a promised land of 'milk and honey' from which I was 'exiled'.

Chapter I
Early August 1995
in Northern Dalmatia, Croatia

The war was raging with full might and destructive power. Deafening explosions were echoing from the nearby mountains. The grey, mountainous rocks were breaking under the impact of the shelling. Suddenly silence, yes, just like in a dream, tricking your mind that everything is well and fine. The temporary peace is quickly disturbed by sound of the war, more detonations, more shooting and shelling.

It was an ordinary summer's early morning, only it was not so ordinary this time. The nature so fresh and fragrant was bathing in the morning sun but as time was progressing the smell of burnt trees, houses, cars, tractors and entire villages were replacing it quickly and falling on it like a curtain. The performance is finished, just like in a theatre. But as this one was finishing another was starting.

In front of you was an amazing sight, just imagine, so beautiful resembling travel brochures showing the nature's beautiful work. Meadows and valleys, mixture of golden summer colours and grey stones. In the background, a mountainous range standing tall and surrounding your view.

These majestic mountainous places and small villages were shining under the sun's glow; you could think they were like ancient warriors never defeated and now, observing from far and not interfering. I wonder why not interfere and stop this bloody conflict between brothers, sisters and families, between your own people who except here and now do not remember where their ancestors came from nor when that was.

Were they cursed to never feel and truly enjoy peace? Perhaps, they are repaying for the debts of their ancestors or maybe it's just meant to be like this, cruel and heartless, barbaric and senseless. It was almost like every generation needed to experience war at least once if not twice or perhaps three times in one lifetime.

Through very narrow paths over the hills and mountains, Vesna was fast walking with her three children. She was woken up this morning by sounds of explosions and shooting. The sun was not on the horizon yet in the east when she realised something was not right and she needed to act fast. She grabbed her children as fast as she was able to and ran with nothing else in her hands, just ran as fast and as far as possible from this cursed place. In front of her, only difficult paths and struggle but she was certain that the only thing she was able to do was to run and attempt saving her children and herself.

On her face cold sweat and tears were falling together, falling on the land that she loved so dearly. Like in a nightmare well-known pictures were rolling in front of her eyes like a movie. Her thoughts were on her children, her husband, her home which will start burning at any minute, her dear home which she built together with her husband so their family could live there happily.

She stumbled upon a rock on her way and almost lost her balance with her son in her arms. Vesna was carrying her youngest son, Milan. He was three and a half years old and looked like his father Nikola. He was able to walk but Vesna was worried he would hurt himself whilst moving through the narrow rugged and uneven paths. She held him tightly in her arms and pushed through as fast as she was able to.

A strength unknown to her woke up inside her and her heart was beating fast and loud, she was able to hear it and feel it all over her body. Milan didn't speak at all, only looked around in fear or maybe in awe trying to remember the dear places, his village, his childhood which had only started. His eyes were big and filled with tears, looking in the direction of the home village as if he would never see it again as if it was his last day on this earth. In a moment frozen in time as if a young man was behind those dark eyes, a man able to understand the heaviness of this moment.

Next to Vesna on her right was Igor, her six-year-old son. He was moving swiftly and skilfully through the narrow paths. He was not aware of the moment, he was just running but did not know why and where it was like a game as if they were chased by wild animals, Vesna thought she wouldn't mind fighting the animals at all.

Igor, like his bother Milan looked like Nikola, Vesna's 33-year-old husband. Igor's eyes were shiny brown and his hair light brown and in places almost blond and curly. He was moving next to Vesna and at times in front of her, but when the sound of shotting and shelling would surprise him, he would grab his mother's hand in panic as if surprised and startled.

In front of them by several metres was Tina, Vesna's oldest child and the only one resembling her mother's look. She was fast and skilful as if she knew the terrain perfectly and was already practising this flight before. She was 9 years old but mature and smart as if well beyond her years. Tina was aware of the situation and understood there was a civil war in her country. Her people were fighting each other since she could remember and fight was coming to an end. The war started 4 years ago when she was only five.

She could not remember the peace nor prosperity but only war which lasted forever in her mind. Her big dark brown eyes were filled with fear, her black like coal hair was tied in a ponytail and jumping from side to side as she was moving left and right through the small paths. Like a goat finding its way through the small bushes and jumping over smaller stones, she was strong and not giving up. At times she would be so far from her mother and brothers, she would stop briefly and wait for them to catch up.

Vesna was struggling and as time was passing, was becoming very tired and thirsty. Tears were falling down her face so fast as rivers full of fresh water. She was asking herself what was happening and why was she in this situation but there were no answers. Her home was at the end of the village and it appears others did not tell her about civilians fleeing the area since the conflict deteriorated between the two warring sides. Her husband was mobilised and taken to war as all other able-bodied males were and she was left at home with three children.

Vesna was from the same village, but she fell in love with Nikola when she was still a teenager. They married when she was only 18 years old after she finished high school and after he returned from serving the compulsory army service in Yugoslavia. The distance between them which lasted 14 months whilst Nikola was in the army only strengthened their resolve to unite in marriage on his return and start a family together.

Vesna was from a Croatian family whereas Nikola was from Serbian. Croats and Serbs lived in this village, like in many others in Croatia, in apparent peace and mutual understanding. However, when it came to serious things like marriage Vesna's parents wanted her to marry a Croatian person, but she did not listen.

"We will never give you our blessing, Vesna; the day you leave to marry that man you will lose your family. Is that the life you want for yourself? To be cut off from your family and disowned!" the sharp words of her father cut her soul like razor wire.

"Please, father, please if you only allow you will see Nikola is a great man, you will like him I am sure," pleaded Vesna.

"If he was the last man on this earth, I would still not give you my blessing. Think carefully about what you will lose, think carefully, Vesna, before you can change. In time, you will find a good and honest Croatian man and have a family with him. This day will not even be in your memory. Think carefully, Vesna!" he yelled with anger in his voice and disappointment in his heart.

He was not able to accept, no matter what she said, no matter her explanations, he could not understand.

With a heavy heart, she made her choice. She chose Nikola. But it wasn't easy to do that, a part of her had to die in order to be reborn again and restart the new life. She believed her heart and was not prepared to reason as she was not able to love according to someone's ethnicity or race but her love connection to that person. Secretly, she hoped maybe in time her father will change, maybe his heart would soften, she had to hope that words he said were in anger and that deep down he did love her.

Nikola was same, his parents wanted another girl for him and Serbian if possible although they accepted her once it was too late. By marrying into a Serbian family, she herself in a way became one of them as going forward in the marriage only her husband's traditions and customs would be followed and she would carry his surname. Vesna did not mind and chose to see similarities and ignore any differences. She thought at the end we are all human and speak the same language and they followed Christian religion.

She was positive and thought love would win, it must, she thought. Like in the movies with a happy ending, the good prevails and evil is defeated. Such was our world full of duality where good and evil are engaged in an eternal fight. But in this conflict, there were no evil ones, there were only humans on both sides, divided families into many instances, same as Vesna's.

Croatians were catholic Christians whereas Serbs were orthodox Christians. The language they spoke was same or very similar with only some dialect differences, however still easily understood by all. Customs and culture were also quite similar, especially with younger families who were modernised and already given up on some older cultural practices. Vesna's parents and wider family were against her union with Nikola and tried everything to stop it. But when they were not able to stop the union, they responded emotionally as disappointed and cut off all their ties with their daughter and sister.

Overnight, she lost her loved ones just because she dared to open her heart to someone her parents did not accept. Vesna hoped that once children came her parents would change but this was not meant to happen. Then this cruel and bloody war started and it was too late for their relationship to be improved between her and her family, she knew it was way too late when her family left the village and fled into another nearby town which was under the control of the Croatian armed forces. The next day, her family's house where she was born was completely destroyed and reduced to just rubble and concrete.

Nikola comforted her during those difficult times. He could feel the pain she was experiencing but was unable to make it go away. Vesna understood she made a decision which affected the rest of her life the moment she dared to fall in love with Nikola. She comforted herself that she had no power to make any change and only needed to focus on her three children and husband during this conflict to ensure they survive. Maybe in the future, once this conflict ends, she would have her second chance to reconnect with her parents, maybe their hearts will cool off by then and understand that she only dared to love.

Who would guess that this peaceful and beautiful country would be wrapped in war and despair so close to the 21st century. Luckily for Vesna, she had lived in harmony and relevant prosperity with her husband Nikola since they married in 1985. In 1986, Tina was born and their happiness was growing. Nine years later and around her another world, so different and foreign, so cold and cruel although this was all happening on an innocent warm summer day. How did this all start and why? So many questions but the answers were missing.

Vesna suddenly stopped. She was too exhausted and needed a break to recover her strength and continue. Did she stop because she was not able to hear the shelling and shotting? Was that the sign she was far from her village? Behind her dark clouds of smoke were rising as hers and other villages were burning in the background. The wind was bringing the smell of burned properties to her. She thought she was far enough and, in the bush, not near any village and hopefully safe.

This sudden peace calmed her down and she felt a need for rest. The sun was now burning over them and it was becoming very hot and dry. Vesna found an old plastic bottle on their day and kept it with her to hopefully find some water. The thirst was felt so intensely by all of them and they desperately needed to drink.

Vesna's house was at the end of the village, her husband mobilised to join the resistance and she was left with no one to check on her. Others in the village left before her on tractors, cars, motorbikes but no one bothered to let her know. Maybe in Vesna they saw the enemy, she was from Croatian family and it was Croatian army attacking, they won't touch their own, perhaps they thought. But Vesna was not so sure and wanted to find other civilians who were fleeing to join them and to feel more secure in a group.

Her plan was cutting across the hills in order to reach the main road and join the others who were fleeing and if she was lucky, unite with Nikola on the way. But to get to the main road, she had another half a day of fast walking and the strength was diminishing in all of them. Thirst was becoming their enemy and they needed water very fast. Vesna found a place in a shade under a big oak tree and sat down putting Milan on the grass as well. Igor sat next to his mother, but Tina went to look around. She took the empty plastic water bottle with her.

"I will go to check if there is any water around," Tina said with determination in her voice.

"Don't, it's too dangerous and you could get lost in this wilderness; please don't, just sit down with us to rest briefly and then we will continue together looking for water."

"Don't worry I will be fast and careful. I will only check nearby and if I find nothing, I will be back. Please don't worry," she said as she was running away.

Vesna wanted to get up and run after her but had no strength left. Her body felt numb and in pain. She closed her eyes and hugged her two boys tightly. She trusted her Tina would not do anything wrong. Her brave daughter was smart.

Tina moved around fast looking behind every bush but there was no sign of water. She was moving further and further away from her family thinking water must be close but still nothing.

"Mum will understand, I tried to find water, but I just can't because there is no water anywhere nearby. Once we join other refugees, someone will give us some water. It will be much better when we join the larger group, we will feel safer as well."

She decided to turn back. As she thought of turning back, she suddenly heard a noise. This startled her and she jumped behind a large bush to hide. She pushed herself deep inside the bush scratching her arms and legs in the process. Once inside the bush, she was listening again for any noise but could not hear anything.

She thought it could have not been her family as she was far and it sounded like a man's voice. She listened carefully and intensively for any new sounds or noises, but nothing was there. She still stayed inside the bush as if not sure what she heard and to make sure no one was coming towards her. As she was not able to hear anything anymore, she comforted herself that she must have only imagined it. She felt tiredness as if she could fall asleep whilst waiting here. She thought she should have stayed with her mother to get some rest and then continue towards the main road exit.

Suddenly she could hear someone walking, she could hear the steps so she pushed herself deeper inside the bush. The fear so great that it could not be described with words entered her body and she could feel herself shivering. Was this happening or was she imagining it? She was not sure but now she was thinking of her family and how to let them know so they can hide as well.

No, she was not imagining anything as now she was able to hear the steps of several people walking and talking. She heard someone cough as well. She felt terrible guilt inside her chest. Why didn't I run as soon as I heard the noise to warn my family, why I am frozen here and waiting for what? She was becoming upset with herself and praying whoever these people were they will pass them by without noticing and everything will be fine.

Within a few minutes, she was able to see three-man walking, dirty uniform on them and smell of smoke. She could see the boots on their feet were covered in yellowish brownish dust. Dirty army uniform pants covered in ashes. She could see the short-sleeved shirt and a sign on their chest. The uniform was different from her father's. She was sure these people were her enemies. Unable to move her body and still frozen, she was trying to think what to do next and how to do it.

After a while, she got out of her hiding spot and started returning back to where she left her mother and two brothers. She was praying to God to protect her family from those people and to direct them far from them to save them. Tina prayed in her mind and begged for a sign of a miracle.

Tina was able to see her family still in the same spot where she left them sitting on the ground under the oak tree and as she planned to signal to them that she was approaching. As she was just about to approach them, she noticed a soldier and the other two behind him.

She panicked and was not sure what to do, hoping they will pass without noticing her mother and bothers, she hid behind the tree. She was able to hear her loud breathing and at times tried to stop breathing at all, even for a few seconds, hoping they will not see her or hear her.

As three soldiers were approaching, Vesna was also able to hear their steps. She suddenly stood up and looked down at her two boys sleeping under the tree. Three soldiers noticed Vesna standing under the tree and one of them pulled his gun on her immediately.

He yelled at her, "Stop. I will shoot!"

Milan and Igor heard that and got up looking for their mother. Milan started crying and Vesna lifted him up to embrace him and to calm him down. With her right hand, she brought Igor close and held him like that so he could not move much. She looked around to see if Tina was anywhere near but was not able to see her.

Suddenly, fear in the form of darkness fell over her as she noticed the sign on the soldier's chest. She could feel cold sweat on her forehead falling down her face. She did not make it; she did not manage to join the other refugees without being caught by the enemy. She was able to smell the smoke and their clothes were covered in ash and looked like they were the once burning deserted villages. Maybe they were the ones who burned her home.

"Look at them how scared they are," one of the soldiers said addressing his comrades.

"Looks like your dear husband did not take good care of you and your bastards," the other soldier added smiling and looking at his friends. "We promise to take good care of you, don't worry, maybe much better care than you even expect," he said laughing.

Vesna suddenly felt some strange kind of strength entering her body, deadly strength perhaps, she thought to herself. She could not be positive at this moment and thought that perhaps in this battle she will end up losing. She thought about her children looking at them and wondering where Tina was. Her gaze travelled over them towards the sky and she asked the God, if possible, to help her and her children in this moment of despair and powerlessness.

Is it possible, she asked, for a just God to end their lives this way, is it possible for her to win this battle somehow magically and unexpectedly? Were they paying for someone else's debts? Were they so sinful that they meet their death this way? Her face was now completely wet from tears and sweat and around her everything was so hazy and blurry as if in a slow motion she was watching her own self but from outside her body.

She was standing as if frozen in time holding Milan in her arms and pushing Igor closer to herself with the other arm. One of the soldiers approached her and grabbed Milan from her embrace and pushed Igor away and ordered them to stay away from her. He did not have a gun but only a dirty knife under his belt. She was not moving but still stayed in one spot. He stared at her profoundly but in his gaze, there was only hatred and evil. She thought how she could pull his eyes out with her own hands so that he doesn't look at her anymore.

He looked young and strong, perhaps in his mid-twenties and much taller than the other two soldiers who looked weaker and older. He grabbed her thin blouse and ripped it open while she still stood frozen. Her white chest was now exposed and bathing in the warmth of the summer's sun.

He approached her closer, looking directly into her eyes and drawn to her like a magnet. Her eyes burning with fire looked at the soldier. Milan suddenly screamed but Igor pulled him to himself and yelled from the top of his lungs, Mummy, Mummy but she did not turn but stayed focused. The other soldier pushed Igor and slapped him hard so that he fell on the ground and yelled at him to stop crying. Vesna looked at Igor and could see the red blood on his face and indescribable fear in his eyes looking towards his mother and silently asking for help.

The young soldier appeared confused for a moment as Vesna stayed in her spot not moving or reacting to Igor's and Milan's tears and approached her even closer. She took a step towards the soldier looking directly into his eyes and pulled his knife skilfully as if already having done so in the past and pushed it into his abdomen as deep as it was possible. The soldier screamed in pain and hit her across her face.

As he hit her, he fell to the ground. But then a gunshot, directly into her heart from the other soldier. The world around her spun for a moment and she fell down on her back looking directly into the sky. Her long black shiny hair fell around her face. Her body now on the fragrant grass of her most beloved homeland. A strange perhaps a cramp on her face resembling a smile. An interrupted life when it was the most potent, most needed by her children, by her husband.

The soldier who shot her in panic looked around himself. He directed the gun towards two boys and pulled the trigger twice. All three were now united to continue travelling towards the next life. Their small bodies were on the ground covered with their red blood. Two soldiers left the place of the murder and hurried away as fast as possible before anyone saw them.

The sun was moving towards the west looking for a beautiful mountain to dive under and to hide. Evening dusk was falling and refreshing the region with cool breeze. So easily three young lives were taken, witnessed only by the nature around them and by their dear Tina who was now approaching the scene of the murder and tragedy. She walked as if frozen and numb slowly towards her mother first. She looked at her two brothers and with all her strength pulled their bodies one by one closer to their mother. She looked at three of them, somehow removed and disoriented.

"God, you took my dear once from me, but who did you leave me to, how will I be without them on my own, it's impossible, God. It's impossible, you must take me as well to join them. Please wait for me, my dear mum, my dear brothers, please wait for me, I want to come with you as well," she begged but there was no God there to hear her.

She was left alone whilst the night was approaching and falling on these beautiful regions of her dearest homeland. She took her mother's hand and noticed a ring, a wedding band, she pulled it off and squeezed it in her small hand. She sat near them on the ground and felt powerless and weak as if her soul was leaving her tired body. She closed her eyes and laid on the grass as if a wounded warrior ready to give up and stop fighting because there were no more reasons to fight.

Chapter II

It was the year 2010. What a magnificent sunny morning in front of Ornella's eyes. The window of the hotel room was overlooking the crystal clear and calm sea. From the nearby forest, the fragrant pine scent was travelling mixed with the scent of sea and morning breeze. Spain, such a wonderful travel destination, an excellent pick for a quick refreshing holiday Ornella desperately needed. Two weeks went by fast, but she felt she was able to rejuvenate and relax. Although alone, she did not mind travelling and seeing new and exciting destinations. It was a small reward she was able to afford herself and just for herself.

On her face only a smile and contentment. Whilst she was sitting on the balcony and reflecting on her two weeks away from home, from work from everyday life she felt ready to face the reality again. Work was waiting and she felt her 'batteries' were recharged. She felt rested, rejuvenated and eager to return home to Australia.

Ornella Moon was a young and independent woman. She was 24 years old and had already graduated as a lawyer specialising in Criminal and Family law. Work excited her giving her strength to do always more and better, to keep improving and to keep learning. The learning never stopped for her and every day was another opportunity to learn something new.

This evening, she was returning home to her parents who she lived with. They were eagerly waiting for her return as they were close to their daughter and not having her around for two weeks was as long as they were able to cope.

It was 9 PM and Ornella was already at the airport. The plane was there waiting for her to step in and take her into the heights of the sky. Taking off was the most exciting part for Ornella. Many people around her were rushing to get to wherever they were travelling. She did not notice anyone, in particular, focusing only on herself and thinking of her parents. She was starting to miss them after a while and was looking forward to seeing them again. As she was walking towards the seating area for her flight, she was able to see in the windows her own reflection.

She smiled with content having noticed herself looking relaxed. She was a beautiful woman, with most beautiful eyes and hair. So dark and deep as if coming from the depths of her soul. Her skin was milky white. His eyes were big and dark always showing how she was feeling. When she was happy her eyes were joyful and fast when she would feel sad, they would glow with some kind of strange strength and they would wander around for a long time.

Her obvious feature was her long and naturally black hair that was not straight or curly but something in the middle joyful and easy. It was as if her hair was in line with her character, her optimistic and joyful nature. She was proud of her traits. But like with everyone she had some vices and was not ideal. It was hard to imagine or to accept that true love exists. She did not believe that any of the young men she was meeting in her life were able to love her and respect her the way she imagined to be accepted as a person and not just as a perfect figure.

She wasn't in a hurry anyway and thought for everything, you need the right place and right time and there was no reason to worry. In the end, if it wasn't meant for her, well she felt she was fine with that.

Regardless of that, she will be able to find something to fill her time and lead a fulfilling and exciting life. Forcing things didn't feel right to her and she was worried she would get hurt that way. Instead, love she defined as a shadow, if you run after it, it will always be in front of you, you will never catch it, but if you turn your back on it, it will follow you.

The plane took off suddenly, inside her excitement, dizziness, nausea and then nothing. Although every time she was feeling the same feelings, she absolutely loved that moment when the plane would suddenly lift up. It felt as if she was able to resolve an obstacle and there was no more reason for worry. Afterwards, she would feel calm content and relaxed.

The flight was long but enjoyable. Ornella was thinking about her work and how excited she was to return home. This year was particularly successful for Ornella Moon. She graduated from the law faculty and became a successful career-driven woman at only 24 years old. Since she was able to remember she wanted to become a lawyer and now that she finally started doing the job she wanted, she felt fulfilled and excited about the future ahead.

Her father was a well-known lawyer, Steven Moon, who had his private practice. He helped as much as he was able to and was always there to listen to her and provide a good advice. He was in his late-50s and feeling somewhat tired after a long career and planning to have some break, especially now that Ornella was able to take on more work and he could cut his hours down. Ornella was his only child. Ornella's mother Rosie Moon long ago started her working career as a legal secretary and that's when the love blossomed between her and Steven. Their life was filled with love, laughter and mutual understanding.

Ornella was very lucky to have such supporting and understanding parents who natured in her empathy, understanding and developing values which she had used as building foundations of her own life. Ornella was observant and was able to see that not everyone was as lucky as her and especially with her legal work she was able to witness broken homes and lives of many others.

In those situations, she would turn to God and give thanks for everything she was experiencing. Sometimes, strange thoughts would enter her mind asking her how she would feel if she was to lose her loved ones but quickly, she would shut this down and change the train of thought avoiding this thought as it gave her an uneasy feeling.

"In this life, I was granted an easy, affluent, prosperous life with loving parents. I can only say thank you, my God, for rewarding me like this. I will try my best to lead this life in never-ending gratitude to you. I wasn't lucky to have any siblings but that is fine. I accept the gift of life bestowed on me and I promise to be a loyal servant of you my God, as long as I shall live."

Ornella would close her hands and eyes as if praying and speak to the Lord directly whenever she felt the need to.

She still lived with her parents in a coastal town of Geelong nearby Melbourne in Australia where the family had a beautiful house situated on a large block of land. The travel to the city was exciting as the place was buzzing with people but returning home to a quiet place was something, she valued a lot. It was the balance between the two worlds that she enjoyed and being somewhere in between felt comfortable for her.

Her family home was surrounded by flower gardens which her mother Rosie looked after and proudly presented to visitors. Her father was spending most of his time in his glass room at the back of the house overlooking the garden and the trees in the backyard. The land surrounding the house was so big that it felt as if they were the only ones living in the town secluded and isolated from the rest of the world.

It only looks like that from the outside, but the Moon family was busy and socialising a lot. Christmas and Easter parties were often done at the house as well as family visiting and friends who would come and stay with them whenever they needed to. Ornella was the only child but never felt alone as she had relatives and friends who were quite close to her.

But from all, she could point out, only one to be her best friend. It was her horse Silka which she had since her 15th birthday when her father gifted her and since then they were inseparable. So many hours spent together, so many joyful memories. Ornella loved her Silka more than she could describe with words, there was something deep about the connection that without seeing her for a long time she was not able to bear it.

The plane landed as expected at the airport in Melbourne and Ornella rushed out to collect her luggage and travel home. She wanted to surprise her parents as she wouldn't let them know when she was returning because they would be waiting for her and she didn't want to bother them. Ornella caught a taxi and travelled home. It was warming to her heart seeing her beautiful country again after a short break and she was appreciating how much she was connected to it.

Australia was a country different from others, there was something wild and free about it, there was something so unique that anyone from any other place on this planet would be able to find it. It was a place where Ornella felt at ease, where everything made sense, where home was.

Ornella loved travelling but she also loved returning home. She felt fortunate enough to be able to take short breaks and enjoy life to its fullest. Today, she's going home and tomorrow, she will be back at work starting on a new case that she was allocated recently. She had already spoken to her father about it who has been advising her and supporting her. She felt absolutely blessed doing something she enjoys and having another reason to spend a lot of time with her father with whom she was very close.

She was close to her mother as well as she was a supportive and caring mother always there for her when needed but the connection to the father was something else that she wasn't able to put in words, it was a feeling deep inside that accompanied her wherever she went. She thought, 'How lucky was I when so many others were not blessed to feel the love of parents'.

She did not have any siblings but felt fulfilled and not lacking in that respect. The time her parents had for her and leading such a busy life left her with no time to ponder lacking anything in this life.

“I am home,” yelled Ornella from the front door.

“Welcome home,” her mother responded when she saw her entering the house.

“How was it?” she asked as he was approaching her and embracing her tightly. Her father heard as well and came immediately to greet his daughter.

“It was warm, relaxing and simply amazing. Spain is a great place to see definitely,” set Ornella with excitement.

“You better come in and tell us all about it,” said her mother eagerly awaiting to hear about Ornella’s holiday.

“I feel so refreshed and full of energy and ready to return back to my work which I have missed a little bit I have to admit.”

“Have you met any handsome eligible bachelors yet?” her mother asked with a grin on her face.

“Mum, please don’t start again,” said Ornella with a smile on her face.

The next day was here and Ornella was ready to work. She had an exciting new case that she took on recently which involved an affluent older lady going through a complicated divorce involving family violence. Ornella was going to represent her and she was quite excited about it. Not necessarily that the old lady had to go through such a stressful time in her life but for herself given she was a lawyer and complex cases were received as challenges in a positive way.

Ornella will travel today to meet her client Mrs Elizabeth Drive and discuss the case with her in more detail. This will be the first meeting with her new client and if everything goes well Ornella will represent her in the court. The only obstacle was to get to Mrs Drive, Ornella would need to drive to an isolated town called Eastorn, some 35 kilometres away. Ornella started driving towards Eastorn and as soon as she was out of the town, she felt calm and motivated to meet with her potential client and to have a good day.

The nature around her was very unique and simply beautiful. The vast place is covered with meadows and forests with only the blue sky above it. The balance of the green and blue surrounding her was very motivating and relaxing. Thoughts about wishing to live somewhere far and isolating were very strong in her.

Where she lived currently was beautiful and a part of a small community in a town and maybe because she grew up in a place like that any thought of going to live anywhere else but with her parents would always be in a similar place and not in a town in a high-rise building. The young people in her age bracket loved living in Melbourne close to all facilities and many wonderful places to go out and socialise, but Ornella was different.

As she was driving for some time, she felt a bit cold and decided to put heating in the car on as well as some relaxing music. She could see the weather was changing very quickly which was not unusual for the state of Victoria where you could experience many seasons in just one day, so Ornella was hoping that it was just passing through and nothing to worry about. She was thinking she was some 15 minutes away and she would be there.

She saw the sign in front of her to turn right and a clear sign with the name of the town Estorn. She thought loudly, "I'm very close, I just need to turn right here and there I am."

When she turned right, there were trees on both sides of the road and it felt as if the forest hugged the narrow road from both sides.

The sunshine was still able to break through the thick trees. Ornella thought how interesting this place was, unique and beautiful at the same time. Especially in summer, this place could be nice to visit and if there was a lake nearby it could be perfect.

Several minutes later, Ornella loudly yelled, "Oh my God there is a lake." Once she realised the lake was there actually and it was impressive lake to see. "Oh, this is so good she was talking to herself. This place is amazing. Wouldn't mind bringing Silka here to explore."

As she passed the lake she continued driving however not long after the car's left back tyre exploded. Ornella was startled by the sound as she lost the control of the car for a few seconds but very quickly realised what was going on. The fear in her calmed down but not for long. When she went out to check what her tyre looked like, she was worried. What to do now, not just that question but many more in her head as she did not know how to change the tyre herself. She looked down the road but there was nobody coming to her no going in the other direction.

She was thinking she had to change the tyre herself but as soon as she starts thinking about what to do and how to go about it, she would stop because she had no idea. Now she realised that driving the car was not all you needed to do, you also needed to know how to do some simple repairs because look at what happened to her. She checked in her car there was a spare tyre, so she did feel better knowing that it's there and she just needed somebody to do it for her.

There was no phone reception in this place, no one around, no houses seen anywhere near and the watch on her hand was showing 1:15 PM. She was not able to see the sun in the sky anymore because the clouds were covering it. She could feel a cold wind blowing that was not very strong but was very cold and she felt it on her face which started feeling like frozen. It felt painful.

The clouds started becoming grey in colour and she could feel the rain coming into the air. She was saying to herself the rain was not welcome at this moment and she definitely did not need it and she did not want it to fall. She decided to sit back in the car and to wait for someone to come past so she can ask them for help.

Within 10 minutes she could hear the first drops of rain falling on the ground and on the car. She made sure she closed the windows and kept sitting in the car but it was becoming very cold so she had to cover herself with a blanket that she had in the car. She thought how lucky that the blanket was there and now she actually needed it. The rain was becoming harder and harder and faster as if a big storm was coming. Suddenly, she could hear the thunderstorm and rain intensifying. The day was turning into a night very quickly and there was nothing she was able to do but to sit in her car and look at all of that.

Ornella was very scared of thunderstorms and especially when it would appear suddenly and loudly it would cause feeling of pain and genuine discomfort. "I'm starting to feel really scared and need the thunderstorm to stop, please God I cannot stand the sound and needed it to stop," she was talking to herself and as if praying to a higher power to intervene and help in this situation.

She decided to park the car beside the road further from the trees and freeing the road for others to pass. So far nobody was passing by. The rain kept falling harder and harder and it felt like it was going to last.

Suddenly, loud sound like an explosion of a breaking tree near her. Ornella froze in fear, looking around her trying to understand what was happening trying to see if anybody was near to come and save her. She started thinking this will not end and she will not be able to survive this.

In front of her within some distance she could see a cloud of smoke, thunderstorm must have hit a tree. She could hear the tree breaking under the impact of the thunderstorm and the sound went through her body like an electric power. She was trying to talk to herself to calm herself but, for some reason, some indescribable panic inside her was building up, which she was not able to understand or escape.

"Why is this terrible rain not stopping already," she was asking with impatience turning to anger.

She was thinking that she was there for much longer than the actual time, it was 5:00 PM and she could not see anything anymore. The darkness covered the forest and the only lights were from her car now glowing in the night. The rain was still falling with different intensities as if calming down but then returning with another wave. The wind intensified in power and played a dance with the trees around her.

And all this time, not one car going either way on this route. She was thinking even if her tyre was fine, she would still not be able to drive in this weather and would have to park somewhere until the situation improves. She was hoping someone will eventually drive past and they will be able to see her car beside the road.

Time was moving slowly, watch on her arm was showing 8:00 PM exactly. She had been in her car for the past seven hours covered in her blanket and from mental exhaustion, she was not able to keep her eyes open anymore. She was starting to fall asleep and as soon as her eyes were closed a dream was coming to her. She was sleeping for approximately 3 hours and the rain was still falling but not as strong as before, thunderstorms have stopped which was good. Her body felt stiff and in pain from sleeping in an uncomfortable position. The cold was felt now throughout her whole body and she realised she was shivering.

Can this night become anymore worse than it already is? She was asking herself because there was nobody else to talk to, she looked again at what time it was, very close to 11 PM. The wind was strong she could hear it whistling through the trees and around her car she felt a headache and a pain in her all over her body.

"Am I going to stay in this damn car the whole night, I don't think I can do it," she was talking to herself loudly. But then in front of her, she could see a light and a car. Ornella was confused and thinking what to do when she was realising the car is going to pass by. She tried to get out of the car and stop this person who was driving and who looked like he was going to escape her.

"Help me help me," she yelled without any effect, the car passed her.

She returned to the car and she could not keep herself strong anymore she started crying very loudly. She didn't care if anyone was going to see her because by now, she was sure that nobody lives here and she felt absolutely terrible. She was worried for her parents as well because they will be surprised that she did not contact them and did not come back home and she really hated this feeling of powerlessness.

She started blaming herself for falling asleep and for letting that person pass her. If only she was awake, she would act much faster and that person would see her and would stop and would help her. The tears kept falling and she could not stop herself. The body was shivering from cold and tears falling like rivers. She tried to calm herself down but unsuccessfully.

Then in front of her directly towards her face, she saw a light a car was returning from Eastorn and was coming back. She panicked and froze and did not know what to do. The car stopped and she realised that someone was coming so she very quickly tried to wipe off the tears from her face before this person comes closer.

A man was walking towards the car, the rain was still falling but not as strong as before. A man approached the car closer and Ornella thought that this was good, that this man would change her tyre and she would be able to finish this night and return back home.

"Excuse me, something's not all right?" the man said knocking on her window. Ornella quickly open the window, but she couldn't find words to say what she wanted to.

"Oh gosh, you look very bad, how long have you been parked here?" an unknown man asked her while looking surprisingly at her.

"From 1:00 PM today. You are the second person that past me today, one went towards Eastorn 5 to 6 minutes before you," Ornella started explaining.

"Oh, no, no, no, definitely no, I'm not the second, I'm the first. That person that passed 5 minutes ago that was me. I was thinking to continue driving but I felt sorry, so I came back. I was curious to see who was in the car. Where are you going? What happened?"

"It doesn't matter where I was planning to go and what I was planning to do, none of that matters anymore. But please tell me, are you able to help me change the tyre? I have the reserved one at the back. Can you, do it? If I knew how to, but I didn't know what to do," Ornella explained carefully and with sadness in her voice.

"I'm very sorry young lady but there is no way that I would be changing anybody's tyre at this time and in this weather. I would turn into an ice cube. It is really cold outside if you don't believe me come out and check it for yourself. I will suggest something, if it's OK with you and if not, I am sorry, excuse me.

"I live 5 minutes from here, there is a phone so you can call your family if you have anybody to call and tomorrow, in the morning, you can return home. The rain will probably stop and I can change your tyre very quickly. I need to go back to work tomorrow very early anyway, so I can get up just a bit earlier to accommodate you," the mystery man said looking at her with a frown on his face.

However now she was confused, what he was talking about made sense and she would accept it, but she was thinking who this unknown person could be and could she trust him in this situation.

"How could I leave my car here on the road?" she asked.

"Well, 5 minutes you can drive, nothing will happen. Also, you can leave it here as well because not many people live here and nothing will happen until tomorrow. People that live here have many cars, your car would not mean anything to them, trust me, it is true what I'm telling you. You are very lucky that I came by because I can't tell you anybody else would come at this time."

"I don't know if you could understand me, but I'm really scared, I don't know how to explain, I hope you know what I'm talking about," she started explaining, but at the same time, the rain started falling very quickly and strongly. The young man pulled a police ID from his pocket.

"I am a policeman, you can trust me, I will only repeat it once more. I will not change the tyre in this weather and if you want to save yourself from this weather you can come with me, I will not be begging you anymore. You decide, it's up to you. I did what I thought was right," he said confidently.

Ornella was expecting a lot more convincing, but this person was not like most she knew. She jumped out of the car very quickly running after him.

"Please wait for me I'm coming," she said quickly. Tears were coming down her eyes and she was crying although she didn't want to, but it felt like she couldn't control it. She entered into his car. He looked at her and started driving.

"I'm sorry to trouble you too much tonight but I would ask you kindly if you could maybe drive me home it's not too far from here," she said wiping the tears from her face.

"And where is that if it's not too far," he asked her and stopped the car maybe he felt sorry for her.

"I live in Geelong," she said hoping that his heart softened.

"There's more than an hour of driving in one direction. I've worked the whole day and I have a headache and I can barely keep my eyes open. I'm not a taxi driver. I already told you what to do and please don't start this anymore, I don't have any more patience or time for other people's problems," he said quite aggressively with the dose of frustration in his voice.

There was nothing else to talk about, it was the best just to stop talking and hope that this night goes quickly, this terrible night. Some terrible thought crossed her mind and she could not remember in her life if she ever felt worse.

Some kind of fear has entered her body and mind and she had a feeling this fear will not leave her easily. In the car, she felt warmth and the sudden change calmed her and she thought how nice it would be to have a glass of warm milk. She also felt quite hungry. Without another word, they reached the house next to the road. She could not see well in the darkness, but she could tell that it was not a small house.

"We've arrived, let's go," he said as he left the car and when she realised that he was not waiting for her, she exited walking fast behind him.

The house was beautifully designed and arranged with some quite vivid large artwork on the walls. For a moment she thought, how elegant. She felt the warmth in the house as if she was there before. Very quickly she realised that there was nobody else in the house, only two of them. Is it possible that this man lives on his own and everything is so clean and warm? He showed her with his hand towards the phone and she took it with her shaking hands. Phone on the other end rang only once when she heard her father's voice.

"Dad, is it you?" she asked.

"Ornella, is it you? My child, what happened to you today? Where are you?" In the background, she could hear her mother's voice as well.

"Everything is OK. I had a flat tyre near Eastorn but I am fine now, a local police officer has helped me. I will be back tomorrow and explain everything in detail, you have no need to worry. Finally, I was able to call you and let you know."

"Thank God. My Child, I was so worried about the bad weather and all. Were there any thunderstorms or just wind and rain?"

"Yes, enough thunderstorm and rain, trust me," said Ornella.

"Don't worry about me I will be back home tomorrow between 9:00 and 10:00 AM. The man who came to my rescue he's a policeman, so I was quite lucky I have to say. It's very late now and the weather is still bad outside. I will see you tomorrow, OK?" she asked for permission to stay.

"OK, daughter, if you think so but if you change your mind, please let us know and we will come to get you, doesn't matter if it's far away."

"No, Dad, it is fine, trust me. I love you," said Ornella before hanging up. She felt as if this heavy burden from her back was taken off and now, she was able to breathe again.

As she put the phone down, she looked around expecting to see the man, however there was no one around.

"Where is that policeman?" she asked loudly but then there was noise coming from one of the rooms. She could clearly hear a quiet music coming from a radio. She walked towards the music and once in the room, she could see that the man was warming up some milk on the stove in the kitchen. She could smell it in the air.

"This is a really good idea, the whole time I am imagining a cup of milk with some honey," Ornella started conversation.

"Be patient and your fantasies will become your reality," he said while smiling at her.

"I am so sorry," said Ornella suddenly whilst placing her hand on her chest. "I will spend the night here but I don't even know your name," she said whilst looking at the clock which was showing that the midnight was already behind them.

"That's not a big problem. To be honest, I wouldn't even remember to ask your name," he said and added, "maybe it's not important what our names are, let this night pass and you forget that you ever had a flat tyre near Eastorn."

"Oh no, absolutely not, that's not right. We should introduce ourselves. I will be first. I am Ornella Moon," she said and put her hand towards him getting ready for a handshake.

"OK, no worries, good to meet you, I am Igor Savic," he said and squeezed her hand tightly in a handshake.

As he did that, she pulled her hand out very quickly and put both hands on her ears.

"Ahhhh—stop—please stop—it hurts—it hurts," she squealed as if in terrible pain.

Igor was left surprised and didn't know what was going on.

"What happened?" he asked trying to help her but not knowing what to help her with.

"Ahhh—the pain, it's so strong, ahhhh—my head hurts," she continued.

"OK, I get it, you have a headache, I will find some paracetamol. You really scared me. Calm down and I'll give you the warm milk, you can start drinking and I'll go to look for medication. I think you started yelling at the time when I was introducing myself, so you probably didn't even hear what I said. I am Igor, Igor Savic."

"Stop—ahhh—stop—very painful I can't take it," she started again covering her ears with her hands and her eyes became big red and teary.

Igor was left in awe not understanding what was going on. She sat down on a chair and continued squealing like a wounded bird as if in extreme pain. He was worried she was having a seizure of some kind.

"Can this day turn any weirder than it already was," Igor was asking himself silently. He was feeling quite tired by this stage and wanted to rest and put this day behind him.

"Are you having a seizure of some sort? Are there any medication that you need to take?" he asked trying to help.

She moved her head from one side to another signalling NO.

He decided to not say anything to try to help the young woman that appeared to be in a lot of pain. Within 5 minutes, she calmed down and put her hands down next to her body. She looked at him with wide open eyes as if looking through him. Igor looked at her with worry and decided not to say any words as by this stage he was worried she would start screaming again.

He could genuinely tell that she was in pain and that this was not a joke. He thought inside that this woman must be suffering from some illness and seeing how young she was he felt sad. But Ornella as if she could read his thoughts frowned at him and said with a raised voice, "Please don't mention that name in front of me again, it's causing this pain in me. I know it kind of sounds crazy and you are not going to believe it, but I hear that name for the first time and until today, names didn't bother me. If you don't mind, I will call you Mark. Of course, if you don't mind. I am sorry."

Igor was listening with disbelief shaking his head and thinking this must be some kind of a joke or this woman is absolutely crazy. He was very tired and had no time for games. He remembered how she was screaming for the past 15 minutes and now, he was also starting to get a headache so he thought he would let this go.

"No worries, you can call me Mark and I'll call you Nella; your name is quite difficult to pronounce so I will make it shorter. I don't want to give myself that much liberty to change it completely the way you did it," he said with a smile which came naturally and spontaneously.

Only now did Ornella notice that her saviour was a very charming young man. She noticed his light skin and short light brown hair, cut very short like on a soldier. His strong arms, wide shoulders and confident attitude portrayed a handsome young man. Ornella smiled back and shook her head confirming with him it was OK without saying a word. It felt good to her that he was trying to make her feel better given the uncomfortable event just minutes before.

"Nella, drink your milk and let's go to sleep. I will make you a bed in the room," he said leaving the room.

"Wait," Ornella stood up after him. "Tell me where are you from and what kind of name is that?"

He stopped and faced her now staying opposite of each other.

"I was born in Australia and my parents too but my grandparents are from a small country called Serbia, on the Balkan peninsula in Europe. I hope you heard about it. It is a tradition for us to name our children with Serbian names. I was given my grandfather's name. I will do the same when I get married. My son will carry my father's name. You understand?" he said and continued walking towards the bedroom not waiting for Ornella to respond as if in a hurry.

Ornella felt really unwell as if she was going to lose her consciousness, the room around her was moving and she was sure she was dizzy. She was trying to find answers for why she was feeling the way she did but a part of going through what she did today during the storm and before that with the car and her tyre, she could not understand.

There must be an explanation but most likely she thought she was tired or even worse, exhausted and her body needed rest to recuperate. Tomorrow will be a new day and she would leave this town forever. Let's hope all will be forgotten very soon.

Exactly at that moment, Igor called her to come with him so that he can show her the room where she will sleep.

"This is the room and over there is the bathroom."

"Thank you. I would like to have a shower," she said thinking maybe after the shower she will feel like new.

Warm water was falling down her silky skin. It felt good having a very warm shower. As if the water had the duty to take away all tiredness and pain which accumulated in her life until now. Although the water was very warm at times, she could feel cold as if travelling through her body but in the end, leaving her body clean and calm.

Following the shower, she went to the bed. She could smell the freshness of the sheets with a tinge of lemon and her own skin was fresh and clean. She just needed to travel deep into the sleep recover mentally and physically from an exhausting day. She switched off the light.

"Goodnight, Nella, sweet dreams. Tomorrow we will need to get up earlier so that I can change your tyre. You don't need to worry, I'll wake you up."

"Good night and thank you for everything, I really appreciate your help," she said with a smile.

She owed a lot to this young man because he saved her today. Just a thought that she could still be in that car parked next to the road and wrapped in a thin blanket in cold, made her feel sick in the stomach. She really needed to thank this man for everything.

"No need to thank me but get a good rest because tomorrow we're getting up early," he said and close the door quickly.

Ornella gazed towards the window. The rain was still falling pretty hard. She turned on her side away from the window trying to think of something nice so that she could fall asleep as soon as possible. But before she was even aware of it, she was deep in a sleep dreaming.

An unknown woman with a long black hair falling over her shoulders and back with big brown eyes, just stared at her. Ornella felt fear from that woman. Ornella was in sweat all over her face. The unknown woman approached her and came very close, she looked at her directly with a frown in her gaze. And then suddenly started to talk but Ornella could not understand a word. Ornella tried with all her strength to concentrate and to listen so that she could understand what she was trying to tell her, but she couldn't succeed. After a while, she started chasing her away and begging her to leave her and to go away.

'Return my ring, you have to return it, it belongs to me,' the unknown woman said in a strange language, but Ornella understood it.

Ornella jumped out of the bed. She felt her body was wet from sweat and she kept looking around the room not realising if what happened was a dream or reality. She could still hear the words of the woman in her head. The rain was still falling and at the same time strong thunderstorms cut through the sky.

"Help me—help me please—" she screamed from the top of her lungs and started crying. She now felt very cold and was shivering. A fast beating of her heart was felt throughout her body.

Igor came running to the room, he looked around quickly but realised she must have had a bad dream. He felt sorry for her. When she realised, he was near her she jumped towards him and hugged him strongly with all the strength that she had.

A river of tears was falling while she was hugging him tightly and shivering from the cold. He hugged her back and waited for her to calm down and to check what was going on. After a while, she calm down and stopped crying. Being close to him calmed her down. But the dream was still in her memory and she felt the fear of the woman.

"Please don't leave me here alone, can I sleep in your bedroom? I had a bad dream; very bad. I'm worried I will die if you leave me here alone—"

"I don't think you will die, Nella, it's not that easy. Today must have been very traumatic for you and that's why you are scared now. Calm down, everything will be OK."

He put his hands around her face looking directly into her eyes. She was very gentle and beautiful. Her eyes were shining like black pearls in the night, her face was pale and wet from tears and cold sweat.

"Everything will be alright, just stop thinking about the bad dream," he provided some advice. Ornella knew very well how she was feeling but was not able to explain it well. As if there were no words left.

"I was dreaming about that woman and she was talking about something, but I couldn't understand her. But then, somehow, I can't explain, a part of me did understand, that's when I felt really scared. She told me to return the ring and that it was hers and that it belonged to her. She wants me to return her ring," Ornella started explaining but it didn't make much sense to Igor.

"Nella, calm down, please, everything will be alright. It is just a dream, you will forget it by tomorrow. Just don't keep thinking about that anymore," he tried to convince her but as the night was progressing, this was becoming stranger to him and he felt somehow involved and responsible. He felt maybe this young woman needed medical help.

He took her in his arms and carried to another room. Ornella strangely calmed down but did not want to close her eyes. She was still scared of the dream and from that woman but also of something else that she could not explain. The woman looked normal, although maybe a little bit distressed with her long hair being all messy. She asked for a ring and nothing more.

Ornella had never seen that woman before, nor did she have any rings. Maybe she should start being worried about herself, she thought, she did not feel well and some strange things started happening to her that she could not connect nor explain.

On the other hand, feeling the closeness of Igor especially when he took her into his arms as if she was made of feathers. Oh—that felt very good—and so strange at the same time. She could not remember ever feeling so close to any man, let alone a complete stranger she only met hours ago. It was too hard to comprehend, too hard for Ornella to understand what she was experiencing suddenly.

"Igor, I am so sorry," she said but then after realising that she said his name with no difficulties experienced, she stopped and covered her mouth with her hands. How did she manage to say that name now but there was no pain and nothing extraordinary happened to her? There was no dizziness or headache, absolutely nothing.

"What did you want to say," he asked looking at her with concern.

"Nothing—I mean—I said your name, but I didn't feel any headache or pain. Isn't that strange?"

"I guess that is good, now you can call me by my name and you don't need to invent new popular names," he said and smiled at her.

"I need to apologise to you, about all of this, it's too much for you. Please forgive me. I don't remember ever feeling this scared when dreaming, it felt so real and there was something I can't explain with words, something else but, I don't know how to explain. I am worried you will think something is wrong about me, especially now that I am laying in your bed. Please if you could, understand me."

"Don't worry about that, only focus on what you need to do to forget that dream and think about something beautiful and relaxing, that's how you will fall asleep faster. We have a lot of work tomorrow and we need to rest, so please go to sleep," Igor said still hugging her strongly so that she could feel safe.

His hand stroked her back gently. Her skin was silky smooth under his fingers. He felt very close to her as if he had known her for years. So strange was the feeling and very confusing. He could feel she was relaxed and slowly falling asleep in his arms.

When he noticed she was sleeping he gently kissed her face. It was a long time since he felt this close to a woman. And especially a woman he only met two hours ago. Confusing time and hard to process everything he thought. Then again, he thought there was no need to analyse or attempt to understand what was happening because this life is a strange game with no rules. The only choice we have is to follow the path of our destiny and if we get lost on that path, we know who to blame.

Igor's thoughts were wandering and he was thinking about so many things. Many well-known pictures were playing in front of his closed eyes but for some reason, he could not understand why he kept returning back to this evening when he met this mysterious young woman and when he offered to help her in this cold and rainy night.

He wished for this night to last very long so that he could enjoy holding her in his arms. The thought crossed his mind, what if after today he will never see her again and she will disappear so suddenly like she appeared in front of him. Same as the thunderstorms and rain that appear suddenly but then peace returns. Ornella's body suddenly twitched while she was sleeping but she didn't wake up. She turned towards him and found a comfortable place in his embrace. He wrapped his hands around her body.

"What I would give to hug you like this every night," he thought in his mind. Thinking was OK as it felt unreal and abstract but speaking this did not feel right, this was not reality but something different he thought.

Chapter III

Sun has risen in the east spreading its shine over the blue sky covered with white clouds. In the air a scent of a damp nature all around from the rain yesterday. Apart from that distinct smell, there was no other sign of the terrible night that happened yesterday when the rain and storm ruled this place.

Igor tried his best to change the tyre as soon as possible and before you noticed, it was done as if he was a professional doing this for living every day.

"Igor, I really don't know how to thank you for everything that you did for me. I cannot remember a more traumatic event in my life and thanks to you everything has ended much better than it could have.

"Not sure if what I'm saying makes sense. I am a lawyer and usually much better with my words but after everything, I don't even know what to say or how to say it. I just want to make sure that you do understand how much I appreciate everything you've done for me," as she said that she felt goosebumps all over her body, remembering how his hands hugged her yesterday and how she enjoyed being in his embrace.

"No need to keep thanking me, I would have helped anyone in that situation and not just you," he said quickly but her gaze stayed like frozen on him. Is it possible she thought that he felt nothing but a duty to help someone in need?

She was thinking how will she be able to go on without ever seeing him again. She felt nausea in her stomach. Was it possible that he felt nothing towards her? Was it possible only she felt something and he was completely cold and not interested? There was no answer. Igor continued doing his work to get her car back on the road as soon as he could.

One more time she thanked Igor for everything and decided to go home. The tyre was fixed and there was nothing stopping her to go. She felt tired and her body ached all over. The previous night was finished but she would need some time to get back to her old self. She gave Igor her business card and asked him to call her sometime when he had time.

He could not even imagine how much she would be happy to see him again. But there was no sign coming from him so she thought maybe she will never see him again. He seemed very distant and not interested. Then again maybe he already had a girlfriend or wife, she didn't know the truth and felt sad because she could not find enough strength to ask any of those questions, she really wanted answers to.

It was OK and there was nothing that could be done. Her life continues on her road and she cannot impact its destination. Our destiny is a strange journey, it takes us into unknown directions and sometimes leaves us on the edge or on the border when we are left with no knowledge of where we should go or what we should do.

Igor seemed like a good man and she liked him from the first moment she noticed him. He was not someone that would fit into the typical handsome types, Ornella thought, but there was something deeper and attractive about him that she was not able to understand. She thought he was the man she needed in her life but who knows what God has in store for us. All the roads on our journey are unknown, we keep going without knowing where we would end up.

She remembered the previous night and the nightmare. It was still very clear in her mind and she was able to remember all the details including the feelings of fear and despair. Is it possible to feel like that in the middle of the day, she asked herself loudly. What could have that woman done to her and what kind of ring was she looking for?

Ornella looked at her hand, a part of the ring that her parents gifted her for her 18th birthday she did not have any other ring. Ornella had a strong feeling that the woman in her dream was looking for a wedding band, but Ornella did not possess such a ring. She was thinking about what the symbolic meaning of a strange nightmare could be.

Her thoughts were confusing and she completely forgot about the meeting which she had with Elizabeth Drive in Eastorn. It felt that she forgot everything which occurred before yesterday and only she was important now. As if she was the only alive person on this planet and no one else existed.

As she was thinking about this, a thought that she needed to resolve this nightmare and find its meaning was obsessing her.

"It was just a normal dream, but why did it feel so real as if I know the woman."

She was thinking about the face of the woman trying to think really hard if she had ever seen her before in her life. As she was driving and thinking she suddenly looked in the mirror and saw herself and realised that there was some resemblance between her and the woman in her dream. She had similar hair and almost the same eyes. Maybe she was dreaming of herself but then again it wasn't her, it's impossible that was her. Was she dreaming about herself?

Regardless of how hard she was trying to remember if she had ever seen that woman, she could not. Inside her, it felt like something was broken as if something was destroyed. As if a mountain collapsed and now on the horizon is just emptiness.

She was driving straight home as she needed rest and had to recover to regain all the strength which she lost. It was hard to recognise this Ornella and the one who just returned from a summer holiday in Europe. She tried really hard to remember her holiday, Mediterranean blue sea and the smell of the pine trees breathing in and out deeply.

Somehow, like in a trance she questioned her reality and her memories not feeling confident that she was the same person anymore. There you go, this life is like one complicated story, which hopefully makes sense or maybe it doesn't. This story of our life that looks like a mosaic or like a puzzle which you need to try to put together to get the most beautiful, picturesque pieces and put it all in one, then maybe you will succeed. But if you make a mistake the picture will lose its true meaning and you will not be able to understand what is true and what is not.

Everything seemed like a lie like it was not real. Only the fight and strong will on this road of endurance mattered because to live without the fight loses its meaning and becomes senseless and pointless.

All kinds of thoughts were circling around her mind. She was trying to think of every woman that she knew or did she perhaps meet somewhere but it wasn't helpful. The face of this woman which seemed familiar she could not find even in her own oblivion.

Suddenly, she thought about saying the foreign name she heard yesterday, IGOR. She felt cold was entering her body. What could be good or bad with that name for her to be feeling like this just with the thought of it. She was able to remember the strong pain she felt when he introduced himself. Never before did she feel anything similar as if her brain was hurting and it was going to explode inside her head.

Maybe she needed to see the doctor and speak to someone about what was happening to try to find an explanation. Maybe to someone else none of this would make much sense but for her, there was something much deeper something just not right. She needed an explanation maybe only a doctor would understand the feelings and experiences.

What happened to me so suddenly? It doesn't make any sense and I don't get it. I can feel something cold, something like death has entered my body and I'm no longer myself. I need to find answers, I need to speak to someone about this- she was talking loudly to herself whilst driving back home.

When she arrived home, she parked the car and walked straight into the house. Her mother Rosie was outside as if waiting for her. On her face only worry for Ornella.

"Mrs Drive? It is Ornella Moon. We had an appointment to meet yesterday at your place, but I am calling you to apologise as I was not able to make it. I had a small car accident on the way to Eastorn when the storm happened. I will not be able to meet with you, but I will forward your details to my colleague who will give you a call and arrange to meet as soon as possible. Please accept my apologies."

"No problems at all, I was quite worried yesterday during the storm and I tried to call you a few times, but your phone was switched off. I will wait for your call to contact me because my matter is quite urgent and I do need your help as soon as possible," said Mrs Drive.

Her mother was near her listening to her conversation. She was concerned with what she could see because her confident, positive beautiful daughter look tired and exhausted and somehow unsure of herself. There was something different about Ornella which scared her.

"For God's sake, my child, what happened to you?" Rosie asked.

"Sorry, Mum, I didn't even notice you are here," she said and quickly hugged her.

"What happened? Please tell me everything is alright."

"Don't worry it's all finished now and behind me. I do feel very tired I don't feel that I have any appetite for food."

"I hope you didn't get sick."

"I don't know. I had a nightmare last night and after that dream, I feel like broken in pieces. I was going to ask you, do I have any other ring apart from this one," she asked her mother showing the ring in her hand.

Rosie appeared stunned and confused after that question but her eyes filled with tears and she looked very sad.

"Oh, my dear, what kind of ring, I don't know about any other ring but that one which we bought for your 18th birthday, I don't remember any other ring."

"That's fine it's not important I just thought I would ask," she said and went into the house.

She thought she needed more time to rest after her recent holiday in Spain and take a few days before returning to work. Maybe she was jet legged, it could be many different things. Igor's face came into her thoughts and she smiled when thinking about being close to him. Will she be able to forget him and everything that happened? There was no other man she ever felt anything for, was this something people call love at first sight, she didn't know, she really didn't.

The night like a powerful emperor ruled the world. The clock on the wall was showing 2:30 AM. Ornella was tossing and turning in the bed and her face was wet with sweat. She was in the dream world even though she was praying not to go there before she went to sleep. She was walking in some unknown country but in the dream, she is aware of it, it was vivid and felt very real.

As she was walking, she again noticed the same woman that she saw in her dream the night before. The woman was looking straight into Ornella's eyes and smiled at her gently. The woman put her hand straight towards Ornella as if trying to caress her face.

But Ornella moved away, not allowing her to be touched.

"Why are you coming into my dreams? What do you want from me?"

The woman spoke gently and slowly but Ornella could not understand.

"What are you talking about? I don't understand anything you are saying," asked Ornella.

"I want you to return back and bring my ring, my wedding band. Come with me, I will show you," the woman said pointing with her hand.

Ornella became scared in that instant, fearing where was the woman going to take her. She thought she was trying to yell from the top of her lungs calling for help, but she could not utter a word.

The mysterious woman turned away from her and walked away.

"I will come again. Wait for me. Try to remember me, if you try, you will succeed. I don't give you a permission to forget me," she said and disappeared suddenly.

“Ornella, what is happening here,” her father entered the room suddenly after hearing Ornella calling for help without realising she was able to.

He was trying to wake her up while Rosie was staying next to the door like frozen in horror. She looked quite scared as if there was something she knew which scared her a lot.

When Ornella woke up and saw her father near her, she hugged him tightly and felt instant relief.

“Thought she would take me with her, I thought I would never see you again.”

“Calm down please, my daughter, everything will be all right, it is just a bad dream,” her father tried to comfort her. Ornella was breathing fast and visibly disturbed she suddenly started crying. “Ornella, please calm down, why are you crying now?”

“I am crying for her,” she said.

“Who? Who is she?” her mother asked while her father was trying to calm her down.

“I don’t know, Mum, but I have to remember. She told me that I need to remember everything, she was confident that I will remember.”

“My darling, it was just a bad dream and nothing more. Who knows how many more bad dreams you will have in your life, but they usually don’t mean anything, they are random.”

“But the same woman came to my dream last night. Exactly the same woman asking the same thing. Why would she come back into my dream if there was no meaning to it? She said that I know her, but I need to remember.”

“What does that woman do to you, does she scare you, why are you so scared?” Her father was trying to understand the situation.

That is exactly what I find really strange. She doesn’t do anything to me, but I feel fear around her. I think she tried to touch my face with her hand and asked me to come with her. She asked for a ring, she said it was her wedding band and that I needed to return it back to her because it belonged to her.

At that moment I felt very scared as if I was going to die. When she turned away from me, she was walking towards the grave, I think it was a cemetery. I think this woman is dead—I’m not sure, I just have a feeling that she is and I cannot explain the fear inside me. More I think about it I think her hands were covered in blood, but I am not sure—She asked me several times to bring her ring back, but I was trying to show that except for the ring on my hand, I don't have any other ring.

"Maybe we should buy a wedding band and take it to the nearby church where you can pray for this restless soul, maybe then this dream will stop and you will find peace," suggested her mother.

"Why is she saying that I know her," Ornella was insisting.

"Ornella, do you think that you know her," asked her father.

"No, I don't think so."

"It is just a bad dream and nothing else," Rosie suggested.

"Please don't leave me, I think I will die if you leave me alone. Please be here with me.," pleaded Ornella with her parents.

"Of course, we will be with you, don't worry, this will pass like everything else, think about something beautiful," Steve was calming her down.

She imagined she was back in Igor's embrace. In everything that was happening which she did not like at all, he was the exception. It felt like she met him at the wrong time and at the wrong place and that she should not continue thinking about him. What else could she think about, maybe return back in her thoughts to Spain. Clear sky above her stretching into the infinity. But then again, she remembered the dream and the woman in her dream. For who knows what time she started going through her memories trying to remember. Is it possible that she knows this person or is this all meaningless and random?

A new day arrived, but a cold day. The wind was in the air, cold and strong. The sky was free from clouds and clear. Clouds were chased away by the wind as if homeless and powerless. Ornella was in her car on her way to see her doctor and to discuss with him what was happening to her, because she could not find an explanation and could not understand the meaning. No other better thought was coming to her mind.

Her parents agreed seeing a doctor was the best thing at this time especially because she felt tired all the time and as if suffering from a physical complaint in addition to the strange dreams. Ornella was on the way to her family doctor, a person she trusted and who was across her history. Many times, he was there to listen when she needed to speak to someone and help her resolve her problems as they would arise.

Will he know how to explain what was happening to her, she was asking herself, but she did believe that he was the right person to speak about this. She felt a little bit lost as if not in balance anymore and trying desperately to return to where she was just several days ago. But for some reason returning to that time felt impossible and this scared her. Maybe she put too much pressure on herself, working too much and never having enough rest. She could remember wanting to finish her university in time and keep busy with so many activities.

There were many people in her life but a part of her parents no one she could open her soul to. Was she lonely without even realising? There was this new feeling of emptiness which she was able to feel deep inside her soul. This was uncomfortable and unexplainable. As if she was sad about something without knowing what that something was.

Whilst thinking she felt the need to stop the car and spent some time on her own. She noticed a large and colourful park nearby where she stopped. There were many trees in the park and benches where a few couples, probably in love, were sitting while talking and holding hands. The scene looked like it was so far from the city but instead, it wasn't. Melbourne was known for its very beautiful and spacious parks.

She looked around while walking towards the lake. She was walking around the Royal Botanical Gardens in Melbourne, a beautiful part of Melbourne community much loved by many generations of Victorians. The place absolutely looked picturesque as if in heaven extending over a large space including amazing and diverse plant collections and trees. Maybe spending some time in a place like this would help calm her down. She suddenly stopped and looked around turning in a 360 degrees circle with her hands wide open and free. Fresh and fragrant air surrounded her.

"How lucky am I to be able to leave in such a beautiful place on this planet earth."

She felt connected to the land and grateful that her ancestors came here in search for a better life. She had never before focused that much on noticing the places around her and testing her connection to the land. It was something taken for granted that didn't need any special importance placed on it. This was her home where she had lived as long as she was able to remember and it was a dear place in her heart.

Her hand was on her chest as she was feeling the heaviness and pain deep inside. She thought she could hear someone crying but instead, it was her cry. As the cry continued the pain inside her decreased and she felt suddenly relieved. She found a bench and set on it. The air was dry and the wind cold. She could feel the wind in her hair and on her face.

She was trying to remember the reason for coming to this place and where she was actually going. Oh yes, she was going to see her doctor but she felt she didn't need the doctor now, she felt she had no strength to talk to someone and explain what was happening. Returning back home was probably the best solution but she didn't feel like going home where she would need to explain to her parents why she didn't see the doctor.

She was trying not to think too much in order to find some relief from the pressure she was feeling. She got up from the bench and started walking towards her car. On the way there she noticed a couple with two small kids walking in the park. Ornella completely stopped and looked at them. She knew this was inappropriate to stare at people, but she couldn't stop herself. What a beautiful harmony.

A scene like these ones always made her feel comfortable. She felt warmth and smiled. She thought how beautiful for a person to experience that. She was sure that she was right. The life was made of small seemingly unimportant details. How can one ordinary but a little bit mysterious dream stop a person on their journey and return them to a maze. Once you are there it is difficult, you are not sure if you want to go forward or maybe backwards.

After a while, you make a decision to continue on a certain path but now is that path forward or backward. Maybe we'll find out later. That's how she felt today, she did not know in which direction it was smart for her to continue to go and she did not know where that path would lead her. She only knew that she had to find an exit and that she has to be very strong and very courageous.

She felt some very difficult to explain feelings that what was happening to her was somehow very important. As if all of this was somehow extremely important but she needed to solve the barriers and move forward. As if she finds the answers to this question and all of her problems would be resolved. At this moment she felt she did not need a doctor. On her own she will be able to calm her tired mind and body. She was courageous enough and she can do it on her own.

She sat in a car and put the heating on while she continued thinking. The fear has to be eliminated, this fear that was planted inside her soul. There was nothing to be afraid of. No one can do anything wrong to her. Anyone could be experiencing similar things and what is so wrong about all of this to start panicking, Ornella continued asking many questions and trying to convince herself that everything was well.

She was aware that life sometimes can be cruel but how many understood that the fight against the cruelty has to be decisive and victory guaranteed, of course, if we're fighting with all that we have and possess.

"How did I so quickly give up, so easily, nonsense, absolute nonsense. There is nothing that can change me or defeat me. So quickly I fell into the trap of fear and sadness. I will not allow myself to do this.

"I will shove this dream out and then everything will be like before. I'm way too young to be thinking about all of this and worrying. I have really disappointed myself. Where is all of that energy that lived inside me it shouldn't be able to disappear so quickly just after experiencing a few strange dreams. That energy and will is still inside and it's hiding somewhere. I will need to find it again."

Chapter IV

"Good morning, Mr, excuse me, I was wondering if I would be able to see Mr Savic, Igor Savic, please. I understand he works here," asked Ornella confidently.

"Yes, that is correct Mr Savic works here, however he's not here at the moment, he's out on an assignment. He should be back in a few hours. Can I check who is looking for him and what is your relationship?"

"Igor is my friend. I was nearby so I thought to check if he was at work to see him but no problem, it's not urgent or important just a friendly visit. If it's not too much to ask if you could please pass my message to Igor. I will spend a few hours in the town and will be staying in the hotel Europe where I will be having lunch. Please let him know if he could join me at 4 o'clock I will be there."

"No problems at all, young lady. No worries, he will be informed as soon as I see him. I'm sure that today you will be having lunch in his company," said a very kind policeman.

"Thank you once more, you are very kind."

Ornella was walking confidently down the street. She could see her beautiful figure reflected in the nearby shop windows. For a moment, she would stop and look at herself. Her hair was neat, her face beautiful, her tight jeans hugging the contours of her body. She smiled feeling confident and energised.

She felt the need to rest and do something for herself. The only thing that came into her head was another meeting with Igor. Maybe it was not the best solution at this moment, but she was insisting and trying to convince herself that she would feel much better in his company. She needed something that she thought he was able to give her so that she could again feel strong.

Igor woke up something in her that she did not know she possessed before. Just thinking about him would make her heartbeat faster and she would smile gently trying to convince herself that it was nothing. She was doubting herself because she was not sure if what she was feeling was important or anything like love.

She had never before been in love nor did she ever like anybody so the feelings were foreign but welcomed. Was this exactly what she needed at this moment when she was feeling down or maybe this is a good thing and it will help her so that she does not have to focus on her own situation and on a strange dream which shook her up from her foundation.

In a very elegant interior of the hotel in Europe, she felt comfortable and at home. Was it even possible to feel uncomfortable in such a beautiful place so elegantly arranged and filled with warmth and comfort? It was already well after 4:00 PM and Ornella finished her lunch which was quite tasty.

After finishing the lunch, she moved to another room within the hotel where only a few people were sitting. She could hear a quiet whispering and whilst looking around she saw a nice, isolated corner where she decided to sit down and have a cappuccino. The warmth was spreading through the space and the smell of coffee was all around her.

She felt content and calm. As if she was convinced that Igor did not come only because he had some urgent things going on at his work. She did not want to entertain the idea that he deliberately avoided catching up with her. And even when the thought would cross her mind, she would dismiss it immediately convincing herself that she was not worried at all.

And as expected, Igor appeared in front of her looking as if he was in a hurry and walking very fast if not running. When she noticed him, a spontaneous smile came over her face. Seeing her smile was like a hypnosis on him and he greeted her with a wide smile and happy eyes full of vigour and shine. His eyes were looking at her so intently trying to cover every inch of her body.

"I was so scared you already left but, in any case, I still wanted to check," he said and put his hand towards her for a handshake. She accepted his hand gladly.

"As you can see, I'm still here just having a coffee after finishing lunch. I don't know why but I had a feeling that you will eventually come," said Ornella smiling back at him.

This was the second time that she saw him and for some reason, he looked a little bit different. His hair was a bit longer and his face warmer. She was not able to see the cold and dismissive man which she had the opportunity to get to know on their first unexpected meeting.

"I have to be honest, Nella, you surprised me very pleasantly I have to say. I did not expect the two of us will meet ever again."

"Well, as you can see the world is very small. I was here and a thought crossed my mind that maybe I should invite you to come and have a lunch with me however I can see that is not possible now but at least we can have a coffee. I have to admit I am very glad to see you again. Somehow, you are different or maybe it just feels like that," she said while smiling.

"I don't think I've changed much but you do look many times better. I would say much better in comparison to our last unexpected meeting."

"Thank you very much for your compliment and I also agree with you," said Ornella.

"So, tell me, Nella, how are you feeling? I hope these strange nightmares have left and you don't even remember them anymore," he said as if it's nothing really important and as if it was already forgotten. But her look was quite serious and there was no smile on her face. Noticing such change in her caused him to regret joking about it.

"No, No, Igor, the dreams are still continuing. As a matter of fact, I have been dreaming similar dreams almost every night. They feel similar or even the same I am not sure," she said while taking the cappuccino to have a drink.

Igor looked at her but before saying anything he wanted to have a second to think it over.

"OK, that sounds like a worry. Did you try to get any help?"

"No, not yet, it doesn't matter. Let's forget our problems for a moment. It is just a dream and I am expecting it to stop. At least during the day, I try not to think about it too much, I'll be doing that tonight when I go to sleep," she said trying to laugh nervously.

Although they talked about her bad dreams, she still felt very happy in his company. She imagined how it would feel if he would hug her like he did that night when they worked together. She found him very attractive and Igor must have been able to feel that without it being communicated to him directly. They kept talking for some time and laughing.

"Igor, please I beg you no more, my stomach is hurting from laughing all this time, please stop," Ornella was asking for a break as she was constantly laughing at Igor's jokes. She checked the time on her watch and was surprised that it was quite late and that she needed to go.

"I can't believe it's already this late. The time just flew without me noticing. I have to admit I haven't had such a good time in a long time. I think I really needed this. This will be my medicine. I am really glad I ran into you and I know that I don't know you for a long time, but it doesn't matter it still feels good," said Ornella.

Igor looked surprised and suddenly had a serious look on his face as if he was sorry that their meeting was already finishing but he wanted it to last a bit longer.

"I'm very glad that I know you, Ornella Moon," he said with some kind of different strength and sound in his voice. He was looking at her very carefully, she looked beautiful in the dimmed lights of the hotel Europe. Her hair was shiny and her eyes were fast and joyful. He smiled thinking in his mind that he could not think of another time where he spent time with a more interesting or attractive woman.

How strange or weird this life was, that thought crossed his mind, life seemed fast and repetitive before this moment. As if a robot following some mechanical routines day after day without being able to stop yourself and look around you. And then suddenly from nowhere, you come across a woman like Nella. Whilst he was looking at her and thinking about his meeting with her, he wished to see her more often and to continue enjoying her company.

"Nella, maybe it will sound as cliche, but I would like to suggest that we go to a different place, it's my favourite place. Of course, if you don't mind. I don't think it's the time to say goodbye already. We enjoyed each other's company, but it feels like the night is not finished yet."

"Well, I don't know, maybe that would be good. OK, I accept just because I enjoy your company very much. I admit you are very unique," Ornella laughed nervously.

She had a feeling that he really liked her and that made her feel good. Of course, that was the aim to conquer the heart of this man, she thought in her mind. But she was not sure if she was realistic enough or if she was reading the cues well. She thought she was on the right path to get into his heart slowly and surely.

The car was driving quite slowly and smoothly. Ornella felt she needed the car to drive faster, more exciting or aggressive. She was not sure why, but she felt some kind of unknown to her energy entering her body which confused her somewhat.

"Igor, drive faster, this is boring," she said with a frown on her face.

As if he understood the message without the need to ask any additional questions, immediately started driving a lot faster. Ornella was looking in front of her into the darkness as it was already quite dark outside. She smiled with satisfaction and felt very relaxed.

"This is fantastic, it's very exciting I like it," she said whilst looking at Igor who was driving and studying every move on his face.

"I agree but you have to admit this is also quite dangerous, isn't it?" asked Igor.

"Yes, I agree a little bit but it feels good," she said.

"Nella, I have a feeling and I apologise in advance if I am wrong but it's almost like you had enough of this life. Like I said I apologise and I don't want to ask too many personal questions."

Ornella was silent. She was looking in front of her into the darkness while the car Igor was driving was slowly reducing the speed to normal levels without her noticing. She thought inside her mind without saying anything to Igor that maybe he was right and she was not happy that he was able to feel that and notice that in her.

"Oh my God, Igor, absolutely not I am still very young and I am definitely not thinking about hurting myself. I don't know where did you get that indication from, like I said absolutely not," She answered back to him but as she was doing that she felt a kind of nausea.

She kept looking in front of her into the darkness and for a moment forgot that he was next to her. She felt like she was alone in this world and the darkness that was surrounding her was causing sadness in her heart. She was not sure what that all was and why her emotions were all over the place. Tears suddenly started coming down her face but if someone was going to ask her what she was crying for she would not know the answer to that question. She was questioning her own sanity and asking where and why the tears were falling.

A feeling that she does not belong became alive inside her and although she knew that was not the truth, her mind was not able to communicate that message to her heart. She had wonderful parents who loved her unconditionally and she could not find a fault in them even if she focused on it. The strength of their love was a strong foundation for her and she knew that she would take what they taught her with her and cherish it forever.

Igor noticed her tears and stopped the car.

"Nella, what did I do? Have I hurt you and that's why you are crying?" he asked ones he understood that something was not right. Ornella wiped the tears in an instant.

"Oh, no. You have not done anything. I am completely fine, for some reason which I cannot explain I felt this emptiness in my chest and I don't know why I could not resist tears. But it doesn't feel like the tears are mine, it's more like somebody else is crying instead of me but I don't know the reason. I'm sorry if I scared you, it was not my intention. Please forgive me. You can continue driving. I am patiently waiting to see your favourite place."

"Do you see that we are outside of the town?" he asked.

"Yes and already quite far from the town, am I right," she asked.

"Do you find this road familiar?" Igor asked looking deeply into her eyes which was still filled with tears. She tried looking around, but she could not figure it out.

"No, I don't think I know. Why do you ask?" she asked.

"We are on the road for Eastorn," he said.

"Eastorn! What am I going to do in Eastorn? Is Eastorn Your favourite place for going out with a woman?"

"No, it is not for going out with a woman," he answered.

"It is my favourite place," he added but Ornella interrupted him quickly.

"Igor, please this doesn't make much sense," she said.

"Nella, yes, just give me a chance, I will explain everything. I am sorry that I wanted to be alone with you. I didn't think anything bad, please trust me. If you can't trust me, it is OK, I will return you home. It won't be hard for me."

Ornella was visibly upset. She was asking herself what did all of this mean and how dare he assume that she would go back with him to his home. More she was thinking more furious she was becoming but she decided she will not say a word because she was not sure that what she could say would be appropriate. While she was trying to calm herself and process what she was going to say, Igor gently touched her hand. His hand was warmer than hers.

"Ornella, did you ever trust a man? I promise I will not be trying to convince you; you can think whatever you want. I was just trying to show you where I live but not the same way how it was when you were there last time. I thought you wanted to get to know me.

"I can see you do have some kind of problems; I know you haven't been working and something's going on. You look like you are disappointed with something. I thought you would like to spend more time with me. You are very special to me and I would not do anything to hurt you. Remember the night we spent together, if I had any bad intentions, you would have already known that."

"I think I'm a good person who lives in his own world and if I'm being honest, I don't have too many people around me because I don't have a need for a lot of friends. Nowadays finding a true friend is not easy. My experience with friends and partners so far has not been the best. It hasn't been easy to surround yourself with people that you can trust. I completely understand how you feel and I agree with you.

"In a way I am glad that you reacted in this way because there are too many people in this world that we cannot trust. I know about these things because I am faced with it through my work on daily basis. This world can be very evil. We live too fast and everything is circling around money and sex. You either join them or you isolate yourself and live in your own world."

"I am happy this way, I am not complaining. If I wanted a different life, I would have had it because I can have it. I don't beg anyone for anything but now I will do that."

"No please don't ask me for anything," Ornella interrupted him.

He slowly started driving forwards. The car was driving through the night full of freshness. Igor drove safely but with a worrying expression on his face. Ornella was almost not present in the moment as if she was walking through some different unknown places. Suddenly, she felt a powerful energy entering her body and warmth painting her cheeks. Almost like a wave of happiness splashing onto the coast of her dreams. A smile on her face as if drunk in the moment and she felt so heavy not able to lift her arm.

But then in front of them, in front of the car, she was clearly able to see a woman standing on the road. Her arms spread as if calling for someone. All of this happened in milliseconds and a very powerful sound broke through the space and Ornella clearly heard the calling.

"Tinaaaa." Like an explosion in Ornella's head she was able to hear the name.

"Igor, be careful, you will run over her, help me," she started yelling from the top of her lungs visibly disturbed and panicking. Igor was confused for a second but once realising what was happening, he quickly and skilfully pushed her away as she was leaning over and trying to get to the wheel.

He stopped the car as soon as he was able to stop it safely. He was not able to catch his breath before she quickly ran out of the car. He ran after her as fast as he was able to.

"Ornella, what is going on?" He was running after her and asking questions to try to make sense of the situation.

"Now, where is she, did she disappear? How? She was here, I saw her clearly. You could have killed her! She was standing on the road in front of the car. Why didn't you stop? You could have killed her!" she kept repeating and looking around to see where the woman was but there was nobody there to be seen.

"Ornella, there was nobody on the road, absolutely nobody, maybe you were dreaming. I am worried about this behaviour. Please try to calm down and come back into the car. You can see yourself there is no one here," Igor tried to calm her down.

"Listen to me, Igor, I'm not crazy. Please, you need to understand that. I saw a woman standing in the middle of the road clearly. Her hands were spread and she was calling a name, oh yes, I remember the name, it was TINA," she said and returned back towards the car.

Igor was looking at her and not believing what was going on as none of it made any sense. He was able to see Ornella was believing in what she was saying but he was not able to see nor feel the same.

Igor got into the car and started deriving towards the Eastorn again. Both were silent. There was nothing left to be said. The evening started positively and they had fun but as the time was progressing the situation was becoming more and more tense between them.

"I am sorry but I need to ask you to return me back home if you could please," that was all she was able to utter.

"Of course, I will. I feel responsible for what happened."

Ornella was not able to fall asleep for a long time. Her mind was racing around thinking of various things but if anyone was going to ask her what she was thinking about she wouldn't be able to answer. Or maybe she would, maybe she was thinking about Igor. She did feel quite sad for not being able to enjoy his company for a bit longer.

Thoughts about the latest developments involving her were also coming to her mind. Without a doubt she will go tomorrow to the doctors to see if there is any medical explanation for what was happening. Ornella was hoping that it will be explained and did not want to think that the answer she will get from the doctor will be negative. How quickly things changed in her life in just few days, but it felt as if several years passed by.

The woman with her arms spread widely was calling someone, but who was that Ornella was asking. A strange thought crossed her mind and she asked herself if she was maybe seeing into another dimension, into another timeline. Maybe the sky computer was broken and now we can't tell what's right and what's wrong. That mystery caused in her indescribable curiosity but also anxiety.

She was scared from the dream and she was scared from the night. But the night was like an emperor ruling over its subjects while Ornella was worried if she would ever see the light of the day. She felt pessimistic exhausted and simply sad. As if someone else, someone different from her was living inside her but she did not recognise that person and she did not understand her.

In some moments she thought she does not even recognise or understand herself. She tried not to think about this anymore because it made her even sadder and even more stressed. She remembered that trick from her childhood which she used when she couldn't fall asleep. She closed her eyes and wondered throughout her thoughts doing things that made her happy until she would feel tired and drift deeply into her dream world. She closed her eyes and tried thinking again about her recent holiday in Spain.

But her thoughts did not want to go there but went even further from her consciousness. It was a sunny day in front of her eyes and beautiful orchards in flower, very sweet fragrant smell in the air was surrounding her. She could hear distinctly the buzzing of the bees and the song of the birds. Ornella wished to see herself in a mirror because she was not sure that it was her.

In front of her eyes, there was a large palace like the ones you see in movies. She came as close as she was able to but felt fear as if her place was not there. Despite feeling like that she pushed through and went there.

On the terrace, there was a man sitting but his clothes looked very strange. He noticed her as she was approaching.

"Ana, what are you doing there? Come over here to talk to me a little bit. Did you see Marco today?" the elderly man asked her.

His silver hair was shiny in the strong sun. His white clothes were quite strange. Ornella realised that looked like the clothes actors were wearing in the old Roman movies.

"Oh God," she thought in her mind. "Where am I now?" another question but no answer.

A woman in red thin dress that was sitting very tight around her body came to meet the old man. She had volumes of black hair which was sitting in a long ponytail very neatly arranged. Ornella was not able to recognise her, but deep down she had an understanding that this woman was indeed her. Moreover, she was certain of only one thing and that was this was not a dream. She felt comfortable and a thought crossed her mind how she would not mind staying here for much longer.

But then she remembered, the old man called her by another name, Ana.

"That is not my name," she thought but decided not to say anything. She climbed up the stone steps and went to meet the elderly man. He was old but his face was very gentle and trustworthy. Although she did not recognise this person, she felt deep in her heart that she already knows him. He was not even remotely resembling her father, Steve, but she felt that he was hidden behind a different face.

"Dad, you look different today," said Ornella waiting for his response curiously.

"Oh, my child, how nice is it to hear that. It is like the most melodic song for my old soul. It is like medicine for me. You know how long I've been waiting to get a legal document accepting you as my child, my daughter and forever deleting the title of slave. You know how much I want that and how much I am trying to make this happen. But I am scared that my strength will wane and I will not be able to succeed before I leave this world.

"It is like a nightmare for me because I know that your destiny will not be easy. Who knows where they would sell you and to who? This horrible law! Why do men come up with such laws I can never find answers to it. But not to worry, my child, I have promises from very influential people, the ones that can do anything you want and that is why I am positive and hopeful. My Ana, you mean the whole world to me. All that your eye can see here will one day be yours. I have arranged it already. That is my promise to you and I will make sure I keep my promise," old man embraced her tightly.

Ornella was not able to connect this scene to a whole picture. What was this old man talking about? He took her hand and started going down the steps. In front of their garden full of colourful flowers and beyond the garden, orchard trees in flower. The old man was not letting go of her hand from his strong hold like a cramp unable to let go.

Ornella thought what a strange and unusual dream she was in but still choose to stay in it and not wake up. She was not prepared to leave this dear old man now. She wanted to be with him longer. From his deep blue eyes, love was radiating. But why and what for she did not know. The old man as if he felt her insecurity and disbelief said:

"My dear child. You look at me as if you did not understand my worry. As if you don't know what pains me greatly and deeply my dear. I know you worry too much as well but please don't. You know that the old Genova did not give his word for nothing. I gave you the promise the same day I found you alone and scared, you were like a scared lamb in the forest full of wolves," he squeezed her hand stronger.

"I knew even then that a new day will rise and that you will carry my name as my child, but I still have not succeeded to make it happen. You can see, my child, that years are passing and with every day, I am weaker and my hold on this world is weaker from day to day. Now, you are a grown-up young woman and I am sure you want to live this life but because of me you still can't. Because of me, you are still waiting for that piece of paper which will give you a chance to have a life you deserve. I will not give up and will keep fighting until my last breath to give you what you as a human being deserve, a freedom."

"Don't worry too much, it's not good for your health," Ornella advised him after seeing how worried and stressed he was. As she said that she felt his grip on her hand was becoming weaker in strength and this confused her somewhat. She looked into his eyes and squeezed his hand stronger.

"Don't give up, father, don't leave me here alone. My life without you don't have any sense. Squeeze my hand," she screamed through the tears like a wounded lamb. The old Genova looked into her eyes but could not say a word as if he was not able to anymore. Ornella felt hot tears on her face, falling like a river. The old man did not move from the spot, he only kept looking with his deep eyes coloured like seas surrounding them in the distances or the sky above them.

A voice was heard coming from the direction of the house and soon a young man was visible running towards them with something in his hand.

"Ana, it finally arrived, it finally arrived," he was yelling whilst running.

Ornella for a moment took her gaze from the old man and looked towards the young one who was running and carrying something. Although she had never seen him before she was certain he was her future, her love and her desire. Whilst still strongly holding the hand of the old man she smiled back towards the young man curiously awaiting to find out what had happened to excite him so much.

The young man grabbed her vigorously and took her into a fast spin laughing and calling her name. The whole world spun around in a very exhilarating and satisfying feeling.

"There are no other barriers on your path my love, nothing can stop us now, I promise you. From now on, your past will stay exactly there and the new life will begin, a new exciting and FREE life is starting for us my only one." His voice was echoing from the far away mountains which surrounded them from all sides in the distance.

Ornella was spinning in the circle of happiness, feeling the joy which had no limits. But then suddenly she looked for the old man to share the happiness with him, but he was laying on the floor with his face directed towards the sky. On his face, a smile like a cramp frozen and his eyes widely opened looking towards the blue sky.

Ornella once realising freed herself from Marco's embrace and rushed towards the old Genova. Inside him, there was no more life left. Ornella's face frowned and a pain sharp like a knife was felt inside her body. The tears were gone and the river left without a drop.

"Has he heard you? Has he heard that he kept his promise?" asked Ornella from top of her lungs. How could she not notice him and betray him at this moment which meant to him so much for such a long time. She leaned her face on his and started crying so loudly. Gods felt her pain and sent rain to wash away their sorrows into the oblivion.

Chapter V

A very long corridor in the hospital and many unknown people around her. Ornella felt lonely. Seeing so many people around with their loved ones made her think that she should have brought someone to support her.

"Why didn't I ask my mum or dad to come with me?" she asked silently inside her mind.

It was her fault because she refused their support and wanted to go on her own. Her mother was ready to go with her but Ornella insisted not to and now after the fact she was regretting her decision because she felt very lonely. The nervousness inside her was increasing and she felt a sharp pain in her head. The smell inside the hospital was strong and she felt that it was under her skin and she did not like it. As if she was feeling a stage fright and thinking how I perform and what do I say. What can she tell the doctor when she herself was not sure what was happening to her or how to describe this?

The last few days really shook her from her roots and in moments, she would forget who she was really. Some quite strange thoughts we're circling inside her head. Her right leg was nervously moving and she tried everything to calm herself down, but it didn't work and she felt quite heavy and simply bad. She covered her face with her hands and closed her eyes trying to concentrate on present time here and now. But the thoughts were racing inside her head and hurting her in the process. She was explaining to herself that was because of the nervousness and tension.

She continued walking down the long corridor looking for a quiet spot to contact her family. Speaking to her father will be positive for her and she might be able to calm down. Nervously she started dialling the number but, at that moment, she felt the world around her was stretching and morphing into something unrecognisable. The phone fell out of her hands and the whole room started moving in circles around her and to stop herself from falling she grabbed onto a chair near her.

Her legs were no longer strong but felt shaky and her knees were giving in, but she was not going to let go so with all strength she was able to summon she grabbed onto the chair even stronger. She wanted to sit down to get a moment, but the situation was not improving. A shaky picture in front of her eyes slowly started becoming sharper and Ornella somehow managed to get up from the chair and felt better believing she avoided the fall.

The strong pain in her head completely vanished but she felt the space around her was shaky and unstable. Slowly, the picture started to form and she knew that she was no longer in the hospital but in some other place in a different world. She looked with eyes widely opened and confirmed she was no longer in the hospital.

The strength of the sunshine, light and warmth she noticed instantly. Around her a space, rugged and inexhaustible with sharp stones of various sizes and shapes surrounding her view. Mysterious and pristine world hidden from history and left practically unchanged for centuries. Many trees and bushes amongst the rugged stony and craggy place she observed. The green colour mixed with the strong sunlight and warmth. Suddenly the beautiful scenery disappeared in front of her and she was no longer able to see it. A thought entered her mind that perhaps that enormous sun was switched off.

Only darkness and silence around her and then nothing at all. Ornella lost her consciousness. After 3 hours Ornella came back and noticed around her white hospital walls. At first, she wasn't clear what was going on and she became very scared. But her movements were in slow motion as if she was not able to manoeuvre inside the body.

"Ms Moon, you are awake," said the nurse near her.

"I need to inform Dr Peterson immediately," the nurse said as she left the room in a hurry.

She realised she was in a hospital room, but she could not remember what the reason was for coming here. A tall young-looking doctor entered the room in a hurry. Ornella looked at him and was trying to summon her strength to ask him what happened to her.

"Nurse, when did she wake up?" the doctor asked showing his interest in Ornella and approaching her carefully and observing her reaction.

"Only a few minutes ago, doctor," the nurse answered.

"How did she react when she woke up, did she say anything?" the doctor continued asking questions.

"No doctor, she did not say anything."

"Ms Moon, how do you feel now?" the doctor finally decided to ask the patient how she was.

"I don't know," Ornella provided a short answer and closed her eyes trying to summon strength to ask why she was there.

"Was I in an accident, a car accident doctor?" she asked reading the answer.

"A car accident?" the doctor repeated her question with a surprised look on his face.

"Why do you think you were in a car accident?

"I don't know, I'm trying to find out the reason why I'm here."

"We don't know the reason why you came to the hospital. We found you unconscious laying in the hall. Do you remember that? You were unconscious for the past three hours and we were very concerned about you. Can you remember anything?"

"No, I can't remember being in a hospital. The last I can remember was that I was driving a car."

"Do you remember where you were travelling to?" the doctor kept asking questions trying to figure out what was going on here.

"Maybe I was on the way to the hospital. Oh yes, I do remember now, I was going to the hospital to meet with the doctor. I was going to make a call to my parents and then I didn't feel well so I sat on a chair to have a bit of a rest. But then strange things started happening."

"What kind of strange things?" Doctor Peterson was asking curiously.

"Well, the picture in front of me changed and I was no longer in the hospital, but I am not sure if that was a memory or I was literally in a different place. It was a different country where I don't remember ever going. I don't think it is here in Australia. It was a very beautiful country with beautiful scenery but there were no people around, I don't remember seeing any people."

"How do you feel now? Do you feel better?" the doctor asked.

"I feel completely fine as if nothing happened," she answered.

"Has something like this happened to you before? Have you lost your consciousness before that you can remember?"

"Oh no, this is the first time, but I have been feeling this strong pain in my head for some time now and I have felt dizzy, but I have not lost my consciousness that I can remember."

"OK, are you sure that you are feeling better now?"

"Yes, I'm completely sure."

"Ms Moon, try to rest some more. We will speak again but a little bit later. Now, I need your phone because I need to contact your parents. I will ask them to come here as soon as they can," the doctor said and quickly left the room walking in a hurry.

Ornella followed him with her gaze and wished for all of this to finish very fast. She felt something was happening, but she could not be showing her feelings. Things were confusing and so much was happening that she could not connect everything in one piece. Still, the feeling of nervousness and anxiety was strong inside her. But as time was progressing, she was confident she was feeling better, and needed to leave this place. After one hour of nervously waiting for the doctor, he suddenly appeared in front of her and she was ready to ask more questions.

"Doctor, when are you going to speak to me, I feel completely ready."

"As soon as your parents arrive. Don't worry and just try to remain calm."

"I don't understand what did they have to do with this? I am here in the hospital and not them," Ornella was confused and needed more information to understand.

"There is some information that only your parents will be able to give me and I really do need their help. Listen to me carefully. Your situation is complicated and as I've already told you have been laying here for three hours after losing consciousness. It doesn't look like you can remember the real reason for coming to the hospital, so I need to speak with your family to find out more information. Be patient as soon as they come in, I will speak to you again."

Not long after that her parents walked into the room visibly disturbed and worried about her.

"My darling, what happened to you? How are you feeling, are you OK?" her parents approached her and asked the questions trying to understand the situation.

"Mum, Dad, please calm down. Everything is fine. I'm feeling well now."

"OK, then what happened, what happened before?" her mum asked.

"I don't know I think I must have lost my consciousness in the hospital hall, but I don't know why or how. Hopefully, the doctor will give us some answers, that's why he said he needed to get you here to speak to you, he said that was necessary."

Steve and Rosie looked at each other worryingly and Steve said, "No need for any worry, my darling, your father will go and speak to the doctor."

"I want to be there as well."

"No need, my child. I will be back quickly, I promise," said Steve and walked out to the doctor.

"Doctor Peterson. I'm Steve Moon. I'm the father of your patient Ornella. You called me and I came as fast as I was able to. Can you tell me what happened," he asked the doctor.

"Mr Moon, it is good that you arrived. Could you please get your wife as well so that I can speak with both of you?"

"No problem, she is with Ornella in her room, I will get her immediately."

Rosie and Steve followed the doctor to his room. They were very concerned. Their faces were showing their worry. As they reached the doctors quarters, they were asked to sit and listen.

"As you have already found out Ornella was found unconscious in the hospital hall. There is nothing strange about that. This can happen to everybody, isn't it? However, after three hours she came out and could not remember that she lost her consciousness here in the hospital. She thought that she was in a car accident, however soon after her memory returned and she remembered the details of what happened.

"She reported prior to losing the consciousness seeing a place very beautiful and scenic; however, according to her, unknown and then after that she lost her consciousness and remained in coma like I already said for three hours. I will try to explain more. Ornella is having difficulties remembering past events. I will try slowly to take her back to the past to attempt to determine if there is a break in her memory because I'm guessing that there is a break. This is just my hypothesis."

"Doctor Peterson, if I may say, Ornella had a very difficult night, quite traumatic indeed, which occurred recently when her tyre exploded. She was on her own on the way to Eastorn. At the same time, there was a big storm outside with heavy rain and thunderstorms as well as strong wind. Ornella is very scared of thunderstorms, a little bit too much scared and usually when she was a child, we would always be with her. But when this happened, there was nobody around and I think she survived a very stressful event. Since that happened, she has not recovered well and has been complaining of a headache."

"When did this happen?" the doctor asked.

"I think it's been a week ago," her mother responded and added, "also, doctor, another strange thing started happening to her as she started having strange dreams and these dreams keep repeating almost every night. Since this incident, she has changed so much that we can barely recognise her.

"She is very connected to us but since this incident, something's changed as if she's not the same person anymore. She was so worried about herself that she did not even notice us for the whole day, she's not at home and we were suggesting that she goes and sees a psychologist, but we found out from him that she didn't come although she promised that she would," Rosie said.

"Can I ask if your daughter survived a traumatic event in her childhood or very early childhood?" the doctor asked.

"Well, I don't know," said Rosie.

"Please Mrs Moon, if you could try remembering, anything you can tell me could be of help to your daughter because I have a feeling we are dealing with a complex situation and I would like to have as much information as possible so that I can make informed decision in terms of her treatment and recovery. I'm getting a sense that she's having issues with her memory. We will do all the scans necessary before diagnosis can be provided.

"From what you are telling me and from what she told me when I spoke to her, I'm getting a feeling that she has survived something traumatic and that the recent incident could have revived the trauma in her. Has she suffered an amnesia in the past?"

"I don't understand the questions, doctor Peterson. I feel like I am in a police station being questioned about something that is not making much sense to me." Steve was not happy where the discussion was going.

"Mr Moon, I do understand your concern but I'm trying to gather as much information as possible about my patient so that I can be of more help to her. We did find your daughter on the floor and she was in coma for three hours. She's talking about seeing things that are not there and there are issues with her memory. I am going to be keeping her in the hospital whilst I'm investigating, just in case, she loses her consciousness again.

"She was talking about a place that she never went to; however, she felt it was not here in Australia. Is it possible that you have taken her somewhere overseas in her childhood and now after the incident her memories returning but she is not able to process it? Are you able to speak to her about her childhood and remind her of any traumatic event?

"The memories sometimes come in form of our dreams, we don't understand how that works because we still don't understand human brain and it's hard to tell if we will ever be able to understand the complexity of human brain."

"That is impossible doctor, absolutely impossible. Ornella was always a healthy child," said Rosie and embrace Steve.

"Rosie, my darling, please calm down. Doctor Peterson, she did tell us that she was dreaming about a woman that comes into her dream and asks for a ring. It doesn't appear that she is scared of that woman, but she becomes scared when the woman starts walking towards the grave and then she realises that the woman is maybe dead, so she feels extremely scared. Few days ago, we heard her screaming in her room but luckily we were able to wake her up and comfort her. We stayed with her for the whole night."

"Do you remember anyone like that. Has your daughter maybe attended a funeral as a child?" the doctor continued asking.

"No doctor, my parents died a few years ago, but she was already a grown-up woman. If there were any funerals in our circle, she would usually avoid attending but I did not see her extremely sad about anybody. She would usually say that death is waiting for us all soon, now or later. It is life. I was teaching her like that to be able to stand the good and the bad in this life."

Rosie decided to say something else, she took a deep breath in and looked towards Steve looking for his approval before she started talking. Steve realised, looked at her and nodded in approval.

"You can say it, Rosie. Maybe if the doctor knows everything, he will be able to help our daughter."

"You know doctor—"

"Doctor Peterson," a nurse ran into the room and interrupted Rosie.

"She lost consciousness again, she's in coma. Please come with me quickly."

Steve and Rosie stood as if frozen. Doctor Peterson left the room followed by Ornella's parents.

"You will need to wait in the hall, please. I will speak to you soon," the doctor said as he walked off.

"What happened to her, Steve? What are we going to do now? My God, what was happening?" said Rosie through tears but Steve didn't even say anything. He only embraced Rosie trying to calm her down but inside his heart, he felt pain which he never felt before. He felt guilt for not insisting and supporting Ornella to see the doctor as soon as she started reporting strange events. He was scared how this was going to finish.

"All will be fine, Rosie. It has to be fine. She's a very strong girl and I don't think that she will give up that easily," Steve was trying to encourage his wife Rosie but at the same time, encourage himself because he did need encouragement at this time.

Doctor Peterson was returning back and they ran towards him nervously.

"Doctor Peterson, how is she? Is she awake?" Steve asked.

"Listen to me, I was very surprised, I did not accept that she would lose consciousness again so quickly. I don't know when she will wake up, but I want to warn you in advance that there is no guarantee she will come out of coma. I'm afraid I cannot give you guarantees in this situation."

"What do you mean?"

"Please do not interrupt me, let me explain. Even if she does wake up, there is a chance that she will not remember things in her life, including you. Of course, there is a chance she comes out and everything is fine; however, I am just giving you different versions because at this stage, I do not know what will happen. My advice is that you leave the hospital and I will contact you as soon as we have some news. Also, you will need to finish what you were going to tell me, Mrs Moon. I will contact neurosurgeon from another hospital to consult with him."

"I think we will stay here, doctor; we want to be here when she wakes up," said Steve.

"That is fine if you insist. The nurse will call you when to come in."

"Doctor, would we be able to see her, please," asked Rosie.

"Of course, Mrs Moon. I will show you, come with me."

They followed the doctor down the long corridor and at the end on the right side, there was a door.

"There, she is here, you can stay here but don't stay too long. Nurse, this is her parents, if any changes happen, please let me know immediately."

Ornella was lying in the bed as frozen and with her eyes closed. Her parents looked at her. She was beautiful. Her hair was spread on the white sheets, her face pale without the life power and happiness that she always had. Rosie came close to her and took her hand into hers.

"Ornella, you are my treasure. Please wake up, please wake up, my darling. You cannot scare us this much. How did this happen so suddenly and what is all of this about. I do not understand. You had such a great holiday and you came back so happy. Damn Eastorn and that nightmare. Where did that come from suddenly. You never before mentioned anything like this. You were always healthy and joyful. My poor child. You are my everything. We will not be able to lose you, please God, please help us and please help Ornella to wake up," she said through tears.

"Please calm down, Rosie. Everything will be OK. We live in modern times, there has to be something doctors will be able to do. I just need you to be strong and to calm down because when she wakes up, she is going to need us. She survived more difficult times, I am sure she can survive this. I believe in her, Rosie. I always believed in our girl."

The door opened suddenly and a nurse entered the room.

"Doctor Peterson is calling you to his office. He asked for you to come immediately."

Steven Rosie left the room and followed the next towards the doctor's office. Ornella was left lying in the bed.

"Your daughter is in coma for over an hour and when she will wake up, we do not know. I contacted Doctor Johnson from the neurological department of the royal Melbourne hospital. If the situation does not improve, we will have to transfer her there," the doctor started explaining.

A nurse entered the room in a rush asking the doctor to come to the room where Ornella was because there were some changes.

"Please wait for me here, I will be back," he said in a hurry and left the office.

"Nurse, what is going on?" he asked as soon as he left the office.

"The patient started saying something, but we are not able to understand."

Ornella was lying in a bed completely peacefully. No changes were able to be observed. She was not moving but on her face there were signs of distress. She started mumbling some things as soon as the doctor came into the room.

"Mum, no, Mum—oh."

"Maybe she's coming out of it," the doctor thought and went close to her, trying to be there, in case she wakes up. But Ornella was quiet again and her whole body was visibly relaxed as if she was back in the deep sleep.

"It doesn't look she's coming out."

The doctor was checking her pulse which was weaker. The doctor warned the nurses in case there is any change in her situation to inform him immediately. The doctor also requested her medical history to research if there have been similar situations earlier in her life. The doctor returned back to his office where

Ornella's parents were patiently waiting. As soon as they saw him, they stood up and asked about their daughter. The doctor informed them that she was still the same as before.

"I have requested her full medical history. I am in contact with the hospital in Melbourne and at this stage, I am waiting for them to let me know if we will need to transfer her there. I need to know all there is in her case. Earlier today, you started talking about your daughter, but we were interrupted, Mrs Moon. Could you please tell me what was going on?"

Rosie looked at Steve and back at the doctor and started explaining, "Early in our marriage, we had a daughter. We were young and full of energy for life and she came unexpected. But she only lived for one year and two months. That period of our lives was extremely hard and her death was a shock for both of us. It took us very long time to get over her death, if we ever did get over it, I often ask myself.

"After that, we lived without any children because I could not get pregnant and we accepted our fate that we would not have any children. But several years later, through one of our friends who was working in the Red Cross, we received a call to come over. And that's what happened we went to see our friend Lydia and she showed us the children who were orphans from the war in Yugoslavia. It was terrible seeing them there like that. Even today when I remember that time, I feel really terrible.

"I wasn't ready but Steve insisted and wanted to adopt A child. Ornella was the child we wanted. She was 10 years old at the time and she looked very scared. She was very weak and skinny and looked like she survived quite a lot. Lydia explained to us that she lost everyone in the war and if we wanted to adopt her, she would help us out. We were very happy with the outcome and she accepted us really well and never mentioned anything about her past.

"When Lydia explained to her that we were her parents she accepted it as if we were and looked at us a little bit strange. We were surprised by her acceptance of us, but it did make us extremely happy and grateful. Lydia told us that she survived a traumatic event and she was probably affected by it. Steve and I were planning to look after her and see how we would go and if it was not going to work out, we would return her back to Lydia.

"But to our surprise, she was excellent and we fell in love with her from that moment onwards. Later, we could not even imagine how to tell her the truth and we were worried how she would react if she knew everything. She never said anything, never asked any questions. Maybe I should have said something, but I never found the right time for it."

"You should have told me this story immediately. This only confirms what I was thinking is going on here and that is that she survived a traumatic event in her childhood and as a result, I believe, it might be still early to diagnose, but I'm leaning towards thinking we are dealing with dissociative amnesia."

"What is that?" her father asked.

"Dissociative amnesia is a condition where a person cannot remember important information about their life. This forgetting may be limited to certain specific areas which may include much of the persons life's history and their identity in general. In some rare cases called dissociative fugue, the person may forget most or all of their personal information (name, personal history, friends) and may sometimes even travel to a different location and adopt a completely new identity. In all cases of dissociative amnesia, the person has a much greater memory loss than would be expected in the course of normal forgetting.

"Dissociative amnesia is one of a group of conditions called dissociative disorders. Dissociative disorders are mental illnesses in which there is a breakdown of mental functions that normally operate smoothly, such as memory, consciousness or awareness and identity and or perception. Dissociative symptoms can be mild, but they can also be so severe that they keep the person from being able to function. They can also affect relationships and work activities."

"This is too much to process and understand, doctor. I am gravely concerned for my child," Steve said while his hands were covering his face.

"Dissociative amnesia has been linked to overwhelming stress, which might be the result of traumatic events—such as war, abuse, accidents or disasters—that the person has experienced or witnessed. There also might be a genetic link to the development of dissociative disorders, including dissociative amnesia, because people with these disorders sometimes have close relatives who have had similar conditions.

"Dissociative amnesia is more common in women than in men. The frequency of dissociative amnesia tends to increase during stressful or traumatic periods, such as during wartime or after a natural disaster. Now that I know she was exposed to war, everything makes sense.

"For most people with dissociative amnesia, memory eventually returns, sometimes slowly and sometimes suddenly, which makes the overall outlook very good. In some cases, however, the person is never able to fully recover their lost memories.

"To improve Ornella's recovery, it's important to treat any dissociative amnesia problem as soon as possible. It is also important to treat any other problems or complications, such as depression and anxiety.

"I will perform a complete medical history and physical examination. Although there are no laboratory tests to diagnose dissociative disorders, I will look at blood tests or imaging, X-rays, CT scans or MRIs, if need be to make sure the patient doesn't have a physical illness.

"If she doesn't have a physical illness, I might refer her to a mental health professional, such as a psychiatrist, psychologist or psychiatric social worker. Of course, once she is feeling better and comes out of the coma. She will need to be transferred to Melbourne. I will start organising her transfer as soon as possible."

Ornella's parents were in a shock after listening to the doctor in trying to understand what could be happening with their daughter. Something in them that was sleeping like a sleeping giant woke up again. It was that deep infinite amount of sorrow and powerlessness they felt when they lost their child many years ago. If anything goes wrong, how will they find enough strength just survive it again? They were on their way to Melbourne.

While travelling and the road ahead a memory resurfaced and they shared it with each other. It was this same road they were travelling when they were bringing Ornella home many years ago and when the hope became alive in their hearts. Ornella's smile, kind words, laughter, it was all coming to the surface and reminding them of their beginnings with her and how much she meant to them.

Now they were on the same road, but the situation was very different. Steve was visibly upset and was fighting tears as he was driving the car. Rosie noticed that and did not want to add to it but kept her thoughts inside so as not to make his situation worse. They were on the road to visit Lydia and speak to her before they go to the hospital. Rosie pressed the bell and Lydia opened the door, very surprised when she saw them.

"Oh my God, are you OK? What's happened?" asked Lydia.

"Ornella is in hospital. Lydia, you have to help us. You probably have all the documentation about her, including her medical history. The doctor is looking for everything he can find. She's in coma at the hospital and they're going to transfer her to Melbourne soon. The doctor thinks she suffered some kind of amnesia because she was exposed to trauma in the war."

"I am so sorry to hear that. Please come in. I will check if I have anything here," Lydia went quickly to check the old files.

"Poor child, she definitely suffered in the war and lost her family. She was found unconscious next to her mother who was murdered and her two brothers who were killed as well. It is not clear how she survived. When she woke up, she did not remember anything and the doctors who checked her believed that she probably had a long-term amnesia which was caused by great trauma and stress.

"For some time, she was in hospital but when she was physically fine, she was released. Her father was not found and it's not clear if he also died in the war or not, but she was declared an orphan.

The doctors told me that they thought at the time her amnesia was permanent and there was no need to expect anything serious in the future because after this long time, she never remembered anything and she was only nine years old. If this was made available to the perspective people who were going to potentially adopt her, it could impact on her adoption, so we did not provide any of this information. I'm guessing now that this is happening, once she is awake, you might have to tell her about her past."

"Oh good God, she probably witnessed her mother and brothers being killed in front of her," said Steve in distress and disbelief.

"Yes, that is possible. I will photocopy these documents that I have so that you can take with you because it has information about her mother who was called Vesna, her identity document was found on her with the whole family information. The father was Nikola and two brothers Igor and Milan. Her name was Tina Kovacevic."

"I heard that name before, Igor," said Steve.

"That was the name of the police officer who found her on the way to Eastorn during the storm," he said to Rosie.

"We will have to tell the doctors everything, maybe that police officer is responsible for her going through this situation. Thank you, Lydia, for all of this we will be in touch with you. We have to rush to the hospital and give this information to the doctor."

"Steve," said Lydia. "I know her really well and I don't think anything can defeat her because she's a fighter. She survived much worse in her life and I am convinced that she will come out of this as well."

Her parents, with all the information they had, returned back to the hospital to check on their daughter. They frantically looked around the hospital to find doctor Peterson and update him on what they found out.

"Doctor Peterson, I am back from Melbourne. Are there any changes in Ornella's situation," he asked.

"No, we don't have any changes she has been stable. I have tried everything that I can think of but nothing seems to be working and I'm still trying to organise her transfer to Melbourne. Come with me we can check on her together," the doctor said.

Rosie started panicking as she was not able to notice Ornella's breathing. She ran towards Ornella frantically yelling, "O my god, she is dead, she is not breathing."

Steve quickly came to head down and the doctor explained that she was well, there was no need to worry too much. Rosie was too tired and exhausted by this time and quite distressed with the whole situation and lack of improvement in Ornella's health.

"I am so scared, Steve, what if she forgets who we are? What if she forgets everything again like she already did before? I am terrified of losing her," Rosie was thinking of the worst.

"Doctor, we went to Melbourne to speak to our friend Lydia from the Red Cross. We adopted Ornella through Lydia many years ago. She told us that when she was found next to her dead mother and two brothers she was unconscious but when she woke up she did not remember anything.

"According to documents we got from Lydia, there were no physical medical issues and after a while, she was discharged from the hospital as fully recovered, although she never regained the memory that she lost. Please here are other documents that I was able to get from Lydia," Steve provided the documents to the doctor.

"Tina Kovacevic," the doctor was reading the documents.

"Doctor, please look," Rosie interrupted him. "When you said that name I'm sure I saw her head move a bit. I'm sure I saw that."

"Darling, you are exhausted and are seeing things," Steve was trying his best to calm her down.

"No, I think it is good if you notice that. Let's try saying that name again and see if any of her vitals change on the screen. Keep reading the names of her family, her brothers, parents, don't stop," the doctor ordered. "Please leave me in the room with her. You can wait for me outside."

"Tina Kovacevic—" Repeating the name and after a while hand twitched- "Come on, please wake up. Do you hear me, wake up now," the doctor was talking to Ornella.

Ornella after a while opened her eyes and the doctor was quiet and calm siting near her and observing.

"How do you feel?"

"I don't know."

"You were in a coma again. Do you remember anything?"

"Oh—I was dreaming then, I am not sure," she started talking and moving her head from one side to the next. What she was saying was not making much sense. The doctor approached her to see if he could speak to her but Ornella was not able to focus and was continually moving her head from one side to the next mumbling something.

The doctor called her by her real name Tina Kovacevic trying to calm her down and to tell her that everything was fine and that she was safe.

"Dad—is it you?" she asked.

"Everything will be fine, just please calm down." She was sweating profusely and mumbling something as if dreaming.

"I want to see Igor," she said and calmed down. She opened her eyes and looked around the room. "I want to see Igor," she repeated.

The doctor looked at the documents he was given and notice the same name listed as one of her brothers.

"Who is Igor, Ornella?" the doctor asked.

"He is my friend, a policeman from Melbourne," she answered.

"OK, I will see if we can contact him. Do you want to see your parents? Are you feeling better?"

"I have a headache but it's not too bad. I think I'm already used to this pain in my head. You asked me if I want to see my parents. Of course, I do, can they please come."

"Are you sure you are ready," the doctor asked. "I will need to speak to you before they come in. Can you tell me if you remember anything different or unclear? Talk to me about everything that comes to your mind."

"I—yes—I am OK—I think I would not be able to stand that again—I really think I would not be able to—"

“What is that Ornella? What do you not be able to understand?” the doctor asked.

“All of it, you know—I was dreaming about that woman, it was terrible, but the good thing is I don’t have that fear anymore when I see her. I’m not scared of her but it does cause me some kind of disorder in my head. It is as if I can see two worlds at the same time as if parallel to one another. It’s very confusing. There are also a lot of people in my head but I do not recognise them but then, at the same time, somehow, which I am not able to explain, I feel like I do know these people. What is happening with me, doctor? I can’t stop thinking about this.”

“Ornella, can you talk to me about your childhood. Do you remember anything from your early childhood? Can you describe your mum to me, how did she look like then when you were child? Are you able to remember?”

“Well—no—no, I don’t think that I can. That I do remember when Mum bought me the most beautiful red dress for my birthday and how happy that made me.”

“What birthday was that for?” the doctor asked.

“I think it was my 12th birthday.”

“OK, that is good. Now, what did they buy you for your 9th birthday? Did you get anything special for that birthday? Please try to remember and tell me.”

“Oh—I don’t think I can remember—I can only see through the fog. There is a white fog all around me and I can’t see through it.”

Ornella sat and covered her head with her hands as if in pain. She closed her eyes with a frown on her face as if she was trying to see through the fog in front of her. Through the dense fog, she was not able to see but she was able to smell a very nice pleasant and sweet scent. Ornella continued talking and the doctor noticed and came closer to her touching her hand very gently. Ornella stayed in that foggy world.

“Please try to remember, I think you can do that. Very slowly, we are not in a hurry, we have a lot of time. Now, tell me who do you see? What did your mum buy you for your birthday? Is anybody around you and talking to you?” the doctor showered her with questions.

“Ah—I am not sure—everything still looks confusing. It really is very confusing all of this. But I can see something, I see one man, he’s quite tall, he has big eyes and curly hair. He’s holding me in his hands, he is kissing my face and he's telling me very nice things. I see a woman. Her hair, styled neatly at the back and her face is very pale. I see a birthday cake.

"Everyone is laughing, it is a happy event. I see two of them there as well, but I am older. They have blonde curly hair. One boy is very little, he's upset about something and trying to speak but he cannot speak yet. We don't understand him. They love me a lot and I feel very happy."

"Is this your mother Rosie and your father Steve?" the doctor asked.

"Oh—no—I don't know. Actually, I think it's not them. She is not like that. Everything looks confusing and it's not clear."

"Try to remember more, Ornella and go forward. Tell me what is the clothes that the man is wearing. What kind of pants he has and shirt?"

"Oh yes, he has a colourful shirt and pants. He's a soldier and now he's leaving. Oh no. He is leaving now and I'm very sad. Now, everybody around me is sad and the older boy is crying and he's crying as well. Oh my God, this is terrible, he has a big gun. We can hear the shooting outside and a strong detonation.

"Everything is shaking and I think the shooting is not stopping. I'm running after him and he lifted me up, again kissing my cheeks quickly and leaving me. The doors are closed, he has left and I am crying. Now, I'm really distressed and screaming. I'm yelling, come back, Daddy—come back, Daddy—come back, Daddy—"

"Ornella, please wake up, it is all right, please do not cry," the doctor tried to calm her down, realising that she was quite upset and was crying. She suddenly stopped and calm down and grabs her head with her hands again signalling that she was still in pain.

"I will give you something for pain, you will calm down and you will be able to sleep a little bit to have a rest. Don't worry too much, everything will be fine. I think your memory has returned. You will need a little bit more time but I think you will make a full recovery, the only difference is you will have to live with the truth and normalising your life. I am not sure how you will be able to survive this but I'm positive that everything will be alright because you look like a very strong girl. Who knows what you survived but your parents will talk to you. It is what they want, so I will not say anything else. Now, have a rest and sleep."

The doctor felt very pleased with the situation because he believed the worst is behind her and now, she was on her new road of recovery. He was very happy that she was able to remember and with time, more memories will come back to her. For a moment the doctor was concerned realising about the tragedy that she survived and wondering, How she is going to deal with that once she finds out? Hopefully with time, everything will become clearer and she will be sure about her identity. The question now is how she will accept the reality that she was adopted.

The roads of the gods are unknown, and life is never as bright as it seems from the outside. Behind every bush, a snake awaits to poison our hopes. Freedom, love, and the sky are all but illusions that can be shattered in an instant. Unknown and strange people always seem to interrupt our celebrations and loved ones can be taken away from our embrace without warning.

But now, she lay sleeping, tears running down her face like white crystals, salty as if from the depths of the deep blue oceans. The sun shone bright like the roads in her thoughts, and she cried with tears from the sea, singing with the strength of the wind. She dived into a dream that was deep and fragrant, feeling the pain of enjoyment, knowing that her lips would drink the bitter tears many more times.

She searched for an exit, but she could not see it. She would continue to search for a long time. She could love and laugh fiercely, but how, when hope was gone, and all the trains had left? The question remained unanswered: until when would her tears shine in the nights of this strange and distant world? When and how would she win in this game of survival?

Wasn't she like all others, only like the wind that spreads its fragrance through the air and then disappears into nothingness? Far away, in those snowy mountains that are blue at the top where they meet the blue sky, there was a clean air from the wind full of pain and death. And where was love? Did it live with her under those mountainous ranges, or had it been killed by them, or had it simply disappeared on its own, as if it never existed in this world?

Perhaps love stayed there, where it was looked after like a fragile plant, like a flower of the wild strawberry full of fragrance and sweetness. The richness of our enjoyments and the pain of our losses, it was all the same. Everything was transitory and cruel at the same time.

Chapter VI

"Good news Mr and Mrs Moon. Your daughter is awake and everything turned out for the best. I'm confident the problems are behind us. Her memory is returning as well. The only issue in this moment we have is that you will need to tell her the truth and explain everything carefully. I am not sure how she will accept this. To be honest, I can't even guess.

"She's quite tired at this stage and I think we would need to wait a little bit until she is looking stronger. She's very confused as if living in two different worlds and she does not understand what is happening to her. You will need to be very careful. I am hoping that amnesia is behind us but we cannot be sure," the doctor explained.

"Thank you, doctor, wonderful news, indeed wonderful," said Steve looking behind him for Rosie to share this moment with her. Whilst embracing her, they both thanked God for bringing the girl back.

"I am forever indebted to you, doctor Peterson, for everything you did for our girl and for us."

"You can go home now. She's sleeping. I gave her painkiller and something to calm her down. We will keep her several days to observe her recovery. And please she did insist that we contact Igor Savic, a policeman from Eastorn. She wanted him to come and visit her, if possible."

Steve and Rosie returned home quickly. They were very happy with the outcome and finally able to have some rest after very stressful happenings. At least the worst has finished and now, they needed to worry about present and how to help their daughter recover. They were so scared and worried the worst would happen to them again for which they did not have any more strength. They were grateful to God for returning Ornella back to them.

But in all of that happiness they were feeling there was a dose of fear about her reaction once they tell her the truth. What kind of reaction will she have? They were asking themselves many times but there was no answer coming back.

They knew there was no going back and they absolutely had to tell everything they knew.

“We should have told her long time ago. We really should have told her and now who knows how is she going to understand this. I don’t know, this worries me a lot. It worries me a lot, Rosie,” said Steve.

“I’m worried to lose her, indeed I am genuinely worried. Some kind of fear is living in me now and I don’t know how to handle it. There are so many questions and no answers to them what if she changes towards us and doesn’t see us any more as her parents,” Steve was asking Rose but there was no answer.

“Steve—do you see this ring?” Rosie asked Steve while taking a ring out of a box. Steve took the ring and looked at it.

“What is this about, Rosie? This looks like a simple wedding band. Where did you find this?” he asked her.

“Well—look—I think this is, if you remember well, this is the ring that Ornella was talking about in her dreams. When we brought her home, she had this ring in her pants pocket. I found it when I was trying to wash her pants. I thought she found it somewhere so I didn’t want to ask her, I thought she was going to look for it if it was hers. But she never looked for it so I thought she forgot about it and in time, I forgot about it as well. Maybe none of this would have happened if we or if I had talked to her about it and if we had told her the truth long ago. But same as you I was always scared to lose her.

“Now, I think this is the ring of her mother. She was talking about a woman coming into her dreams and asking for a ring. Once there were two boys around the woman, these are her younger brothers. If I gave this ring then maybe she would be much better, maybe she would calm down and maybe everything would finish differently. Do you see what I did? I wish I put these things together before but now, what if it is too late.”

“Rosie, my dear—you are not to blame for anything. Who knows how that would affect her, maybe positively, maybe negatively, we don’t know and we should not blame ourselves. But I think if you want you should keep that ring, she might be happy to have it. Oh, Rosie—I’m so scared and wish for all of this to finish as soon as possible. I feel very tense and anxious. She’s a grown-up woman, I’m hoping she will understand things logically but there is a part of me that is not sure in her reaction and that scares me a lot.

“You know how she was sometimes frightened and even weak but at the same time, quite determined and courageous. I could never be sure how she would react if there is a barrier in front of her because her life with us has been stable and easy. From outside she looks very strong but deep down I am worried the she is not. She grew up too fast, oh how I miss our little girl," said Steve still preoccupied with his doubts.

Nevertheless, it feels the time is passing always in one direction. Underneath the fear there was hope that they will continue living peacefully like before. Three of them had a great life. Ornella was their centre of universe, always full of energy and joy for life. She was never in one spot too long, buzzing around like a bee with ambition and power. Days were passing fast, like thunderstorms through the sky and Steve like Rosie were captured with Ornella's youth and beauty.

"Steve," said-Rosie, "we need to find that policeman that Ornella wanted to see."

"Tomorrow we will look for him, but something is not clear to me, what could have happened with her. Why does she want to see him now? I don't think nice memories connect her with him. That day when they met was very traumatic for Ornella. Also, his name and surname is strange, it might be also from the region of the former Yugoslavia, same like where Ornella comes from. Who knows what is there that we still do not understand," said suspiciously Steve.

"Maybe there is nothing to it, he is a young policeman, maybe she liked him, maybe she fell in love with him, who knows. Isn't she a beautiful young woman? I think she probably liked him and would like to see him again."

"I am not sure but I guess soon we will find out. You know she doesn't really fall in love that often, I am now very curious to see what that guy looks like. I am still suspicious that something else is going on, something unknown to us at this stage. Ornella is difficult when it comes to relationships and that is why I am worried. Unless as she's growing up she changes, we will find out soon."

As Steve said that the phone was ringing. Steve got up quickly and answered the call.

"Hello," said Steve.

"Hello, Steve, it's Lydia here."

"Yes, yes Lydia. It is me, Steve."

"Steve, I found out some information about Ornella. I got in contact with the European Red Cross. We received Ornella through French Red Cross; however, they gave us her complete dossier. From her family no one survived but her father. He was arrested as a prisoner of war by the winning Croatian army.

During the civil war her father was on the side of the paramilitary and once arrested he was sentenced at the military court where he was found guilty for participating in the military operation against the state of Croatia.

“Ornella’s father, Nikola Kovacevic who was 33 years old at the time was sentenced to serve 15 years in prison and he should be 48 years now. Of course, that is if he has survived the prison. We would need to get in contact with Croatia and try to find more information about him.”

“Lydia, this is wonderful news; indeed this is wonderful. I just hope that that poor man is still alive,” said Steve very surprised.

“Well, we don’t know, I am guessing that he could survive the 15 year sentence but who knows how difficult that could be following the war. Don’t be surprised if I inform you after I do my research that he did not survive. For that reason please do not mention anything about this with Ornella until we are completely sure because we don’t know how she could take such a news.”

“Lydia, I thank you from the bottom of my heart. I agree with everything you suggest. Thank you once again for this excellent information.”

“You are welcome, I will speak to you very soon, probably in several hours. I will contact Croatia and see if I can find out anything. I will prioritise this task because I know how important it is for all of you.”

“Thank you, my dear Lydia. We will speak to you very soon.”

“Rosie, did you hear that? Ornella’s father might still be alive. I’m very happy about this news.”

“Oh Steve, maybe if she knew this it would give her strength to recover much faster,” suggested Rosie.

“Don’t forget, my dear, a lot of time has passed since that war. I hope once she finds out, she will not suffer too much. They tell us that the time heals our wounds, at least that is what they say. The most important thing is that Ornella recovers, everything else will settle down in time and we will try to help her as much as we can.”

Through the window of the patient’s room, the rays of sunshine were breaking through the air. Ornella’s gaze was wandering in the distance, questioning what the world looks like over there. The town was stretching far but on the edges, mountains were visible. Morning, was her favourite time of the day when she would feel energised and ready to seize the day.

From day to day she was finding her time in hospital was difficult to take. She felt good and wanted to get out there and continue living her life. Her plan was to return back to work as soon as possible because she already missed a lot. The strange dreams have vanished and she felt good and without a worry.

She took a deep breath in and out, trying to calm her energy. She could see clouds swimming through the sky and accumulating over the mountains. She wished she could touch the soft like cotton clouds. *Oh, I wish I was a bird to fly up into the sky and feel the freedom and breathe in the fresh air.*

But she could not, because she felt some cruel people broke her wings and she was now convinced she only had hate in her heart for them. Yes, indeed a pure hate accumulated in her. She was confused, why does she think this? What is she thinking about? She has to change this thinking.

"Good morning, Ornella," doctor Peterson interrupted her whilst thinking when he entered the room.

"Oh Doctor, it is you," said Ornella surprised.

"So Ornella, why are you constantly at that window. Didn't I tell you clearly that you need to rest."

"But doctor, I actually feel quite good. I am not tired. Anyway, I was going to ask you when will I be leaving this place? I feel like I'm in prison, I really want to get out of here."

"Well, the way things are, I think that soon you will be discharged but we're not in a hurry, we need to be sure that you are well. You have been here for the past six days and weren't really in the mood for visitors. How do you feel today? One gentleman would like to see you and he said he would be very upset if you refuse to see him again."

"Fine, I will see visitors today. If my parents call, please let them know I want to see them. They will be upset that I didn't want to see them last time?"

"Oh no, no, definitely not. I think you acted smartly and I was very pleasantly surprised. You concentrated on your recovery. And you are getting better much faster than what I was expecting, with no complications. I need you to stay strong like now, we are all very proud of you. And before I forget the Mr that wants to see you, his name is **Igor Savic**, he said he's a very good friend of yours. Should I let him in?"

"Yes, please, call him in," said Ornella and got up from the bed again walking towards the window.

The distant places were still shining in the morning sun and attracting her attention. The doors opened. Igor entered the room very gently and quietly.

Ornella did not turn around and her gaze was still enjoying the view in front of her.

"What are you doing?" Igor asked her gently.

"I am looking at the clouds and mountains underneath them and enjoying the view," said Ornella whilst turning around and looking at Igor. His face was familiar but somehow different. His eyes were distant and dark.

"How are you, Nella?" he asked looking into the distance and checking what she was finding so fascinating.

"Thank you for your question, I am good. I hope soon I will leave this place. Maybe in a day or two. The doctor promised," she said while Igor turned towards her, looking her directly in her eyes.

"You are beautiful, Ornella; you are still very beautiful like before," he said and embraced her gently. She accepted his embrace and relaxed on his chest. This felt very nice and relaxing. She felt the warmth of his arms around her, stroking her hair gently. He again looked deep into her eyes, thinking that he has never seen more beautiful eyes. His hands touched her face which was gentle and silky. He wanted to kiss her lips which were red like cherries; he could not resist, he kissed her gently and slowly.

"No, stop, Igor," Ornella interrupted him and at the same time the doors opened and her parents entered the room.

"Mum, Dad," she said and run to their embrace.

"I am so happy to see you. I missed you so much. Please tell me you are not upset with me for not seeing you last time. I didn't want you to see me like that when I didn't feel well—"

"Of course, we're not upset, darling. How could we be upset with you as long as you are feeling better, that is the most important for us. You look very beautiful, doesn't she, Rosie?" asked Steve.

"Yes, she looks like her old self before all of this."

"Dad, Mum, this is Igor. You remember I was telling you about him and how he saved me when I was going to Eastorn."

"Oh yes, we already met Igor. You know that day when you didn't want to see us, Igor was there as well and we met."

"Ornella, it was great seeing you I will come again tomorrow after work to check on you," said Igor while leaving the room.

"Thank you for coming, I really appreciate it. See you again," Ornella said with a smile. As Igor left the room she turned to her parents.

"I will be upset with you if you stressed too much about all these things that were happening. You know I don't like when you stress too much."

"No, we were not, we promise."

"I feel good and I think, soon I will leave this place and I made a decision, I'll return back to work. I don't know how to explain it but I feel like something that was heavy in me is no longer there and I feel light and restless. I hope this feeling will last long. I'm again in a very good mood. I was worried I would never feel like normal again after that terrible night. Tell me how is everything at home is there anything new?" Ornella asked curiously.

Her parents were looking at her smiling and enjoying her company. They were convinced their girl was back. They did not lose her but they were scared that they could. Steve looked at her and tried to prepare her for a more serious talk.

"My darling, we would like to talk to you about something that is very important and serious. If you are not ready or don't feel like it, tell us, we will do it next time. We are not in a hurry. We want to make sure that you are ready."

"Oh no, I feel good. I'm ready for anything," said Ornella curiously as she was not sure what her father was talking about.

"Eh, Ornella. When did you grow up? I have a feeling you are still my little girl. OK, listen to me, my child, listen to me very carefully and I need to ask you in advance to promise me that you will be able to stand this information courageously. I believe in you, please understand your mother and me please."

"OK, say what it is I am ready," said Ornella but now notes her father's face was becoming uncomfortable and his eyes were filling with tears. This scared her somewhat but she was still curious to find out what was going on.

"My child, I don't know how to start and to be honest, we wish so much for this to be finished for once because we don't have any peace, we are very nervous. As you can see, our child, we are already old and getting sick, you never know what tomorrow will bring."

"OK, Dad, now you really need to tell me what is happening. I don't understand what you are trying to say, but you are starting to worry me."

"Ornella, when you were 10 years old, Rosie and I adopted you. You forgot your life prior to that because of amnesia and once we met you and brought you home, you got used to us very quickly and we got used to you," Steve started speaking and Ornella got up from the bed again with a frown on her face.

"Continue, Dad," said Ornella as if ordering without looking in their direction but again far through the window.

"Our daughter died when she was very young and we lived alone without children. Then you suddenly appeared and that's when we felt our life truly started. Your name was Tina Kovacevic and you were born in Croatia in 1986 in a very small village. You had two brothers, Igor and Milan. Your parents were young, your mother was Vesna and father, Nikola. You lived with them until you were nine years old.

"In 1990, a civil war started in Croatia which was a Republic in Yugoslavia. Croatia declared independence but Serbs who were an ethnic minority, they did not agree with that and a civil war started. The war finished in 1995 with the victory for Croatia and a defeat for other rebels. Your parents were on the side of the orthodox Serbs, a minority in Croatia at the time. They lost the war. Your mother together with your two brothers who were much younger than you, were killed while she was trying to run away but you somehow survived and after that trauma, because of amnesia, you did not remember anything.

"Your father was arrested by Croatian army and sentenced to 15 years in prison. I am in contact with Lydia, our friend from Melbourne from the Red Cross and she told me that your father is still alive and that this year his prison sentence will finish and he should be allowed out of the prison. He should be around 48 years old. Lydia told me that he should be out in April this year. He is in a prison Lepoglava near the capital of Croatia."

"So that is it, it's good that you told me."

"My darling, please understand us, please try to understand us," said Rosie trying to get near her.

"Mum, Mum," she hugged her with all her strength and started crying loud stop.

"Here my daughter, take this ring. This is the ring from your mum, the woman that you were dreaming about."

"Ring, yes, I was dreaming about this ring and that woman was my mother and two little kids from the dream were my brothers. Oh God, this is terrible, like a curse. I knew it meant something important, the whole time I had a very strong feeling that that woman had a connection with me. She was so beautiful and young in that dream. As if I can see her now, oh God.

"I can remember her call, yes, I can remember her. My memory is back, it is back. It's allright, that terrible emptiness from my chest has disappeared. Now, I feel calm. I was not surprised at all as if I knew all of this the whole time, I was not surprised at all. And she called me with the name, Tina, but I didn't know she was calling me. I didn't know that she needed me."

"My child, how do you feel now. Can you remember anything from your past," her father asked?

"Dad, I love you so much, you mean to me beyond my ability to describe it and explain it. I don't know how I would survive all of this if you were not here with me. But please don't leave me, don't ever leave me," she said crying again.

"You are our treasure; don't cry, you know we will never leave; you are everything to us, you are our whole life; without you, we cannot imagine our future. You, what kind of leaving you talking about, you know that is impossible, absolutely impossible, Ornella."

"My name is Tina. That name is dear to me. I would like to be called Tina. I need to get some rest," she said while closing her eyes and trying to travel through her new memories.

"Oh God, I remember everything. Once upon a time I lived in a country made of joy and dreams. From the mountainous hills you could watch the waves on the sea, how they are breaking on the coast made of stones. Once I was joyfully running through the dusty paths of my childhood and imagined faraway towns and worlds. I was asking myself if the others lived any more freely and peacefully like me and if they were as happy.

"But then suddenly, to everyone's astonishment and disappointment, the war happened. A cold, cruel and bloody war. Nothing was same like before and nobody was the same as before. Everything changed and everyone changed. People were carrying guns and losing their minds in the battle for survival.

"No new day was the same, no new dawn was fragrant or peaceful. Everything was smelling like gunpowder or burnt homes. War years one after the other were passing and taking with them the bloody toll. Young lives were sown for the happiness of the new generations and for the free future.

"One day in August cried the vineyards, cried the fertile fields and the stone slopes screamed. A whole nation left their ancient land, their nests and flew on the path of sadness and poverty. I remember the strong shot from the gun and my mother on the ground. As if now I am looking at her shiny hair all around her, her pale face and warm blood. Her scream and that moment forever lived inside me and now, I can remember it again clearly.

"I remember the blue sky above us and a very fragrant grass surrounding us. My brothers somehow I forgot and regardless of how much I tried to remember them I cannot, maybe they stayed buried in my subconsciousness.

"My father, him, I do remember. He was tall, strong like a mountain. His hair was light and curly on the ends. I remember he had a greenish army uniform and a big gun in his hands. I know that gun brings death.

"I noticed the winds were no longer fresh and cold like before. There is a different fragrance in them now. I miss that wind filled with love and snow. As if it disappeared forever and does not live in me anymore. My God, through the stony paths of my childhood some other people are walking and I, I am walking under the foreign sky as if cursed and punished by the God.

"Is there anything worse in the world than limitless sadness. Is there anything worse than endless punishment. As if they tore my heart from my chest and now, I am alive but empty and cold.

"I remember being an imaginative child living in my own imagination. How many unfulfilled dreams and wishes? But all of that lived in me under that sky and warm sun. But not even one wish came true and all my imagination was for nothing, but at least I had dream. Now, I don't have anything nor anyone, I am left alone, completely alone.

"I need to visit the graves of my loved ones; I have to see my father. I have to return this ring to my mother and I need to visit my homeland, my lost homeland where my ancestors lived. I have to kiss the land where my first tears, laughter, sadness and joy were left. Everything was left in that land where I wish to return after a long time."

"Ornella, child, please calm down," her parents were worried.

"No, seriously I think, there is a ray of sunshine, a very little hope and belief in me trying to help me in these difficult moments. I understand that my destiny was filled with suffering but maybe it will not be forever, maybe the suffering is finished."

"Ornella dear, this is not sounding like you anymore, you are scaring us, dear, please calm down."

"No, it is OK, it is me, I have to be like this after everything, what do you expect? So many difficult moments and I survived them all although I did not have any hope that I would. I felt limitless pain which I cannot compare to anything, it cannot be measured. Just thinking about it is making me sick and I feel nauseous. All around me lost its meaning then and nothing was valuable anymore. All plans disappeared, all hopes and dreams. Nothing except the bare life was important.

"I remember even the life became too painful and difficult to bare. I remember the days were long and nights scary. Now it is fine, the pain is gone but my soul remained there and I need to go there to find it. My heart remained there as well as my fears and love. I cannot live without that land anymore. I have to be able to feel the wind which in summer smells like sea salt. I need to go and, please do not try to convince me otherwise. Maybe you can't understand me but at least try.

"All these years I have been living with that emptiness in my heart. I have to go. I understand I belong to Australia; it is the country that embraced me and gave me the second chance. But far from here is my ancestral homeland and I need to visit it."

"My daughter, of course you will visit if that is what you want. We will support you like always. When you feel you are recovered and ready, you will go. We will give you all you need and support you all the way. You know that. Now, please, you need to relax and recover. Nothing is your fault and we do not want you to live with so much pain and trauma."

"I know that, Dad, but I have a feeling that it was my fault."

"What are you talking about, Ornella?"

"It was my fault."

"Please stop, Ornella, please don't say things like that. Nothing is your fault, absolutely nothing is your fault, you were a small child. Thanks to our Lord you survived that madness. Thank God."

"I am convinced that I was able to do something to save them but I was not brave enough."

"Please don't say another word, Ornella. You are a very courageous and brave person, you have always been and will be. Nothing is your fault. You are our only child, our treasure."

Another day arrived but cloudy day above the city. It was the day Ornella was leaving the hospital. Fifteen days passed by and she felt she fully recovered. There was no more reasons to stay here. These two weeks helped her to deal with cruel reality and painful past and to collect the strength for future battles still ahead of her. Only one thought was preoccupying her and she smiled gently when reminiscing about it.

"Oh, when is that day coming, the day when I will fly like a bird to my homeland? When will that day arrive? I feel it is near, I can feel it all around me," she took deep breath in and out with her eyes closed.

Energy accumulated inside her was powerful. In her hand, the ring. She put the ring on her finger and it was a perfect fit. It was her mother's wedding band, the ring symbolising her parents promise to each other to stay together in good and bad times. She was now of similar age as her mother when she forever left the face of this earth and travelled to heaven to join our Lord and father. She must have wished to live longer, who knows how much she was afraid of death? How cruel this world can be and what was all of that for?

Thousands of questions but no answers, no trace of even one as if the answers did not exist. Maybe the answers did not exist because there were no answers to her questions. Ornella convinced herself that the paths of our destiny were such and nothing could be done about it. It was like it had to be. Everyone is walking on their own path. Her mother and brothers could not survive the barriers on their path and their path ended.

"So Ornella, how are you doing? I hope you are feeling better than the weather outside."

"Yes, I am ready, doctor, I have been waiting for today for some time and finally, I am leaving."

"That is good to hear. So, who is coming to get you?"

"Igor will come for me."

"Igor is your boyfriend?" asked the doctor.

"No, I would say he is a good friend."

"Ornella, I wish you all the very best in the future. Take it easy OK. Your prince is here so I will take my leave. All the best again."

"Thank you, doctor, for all your help and care. I will always be grateful to you for helping me recover."

"Are you leaving, princess?" asked Igor.

"Yes, we could leave now, I think," said Ornella with a smile greeting Igor.

They left the hospital together holding hands. This felt good for Ornella and for Igor. Only two weeks in hospital did not seem like a long time but somehow for Ornella, it felt.

The car was on the road and Igor was driving slowly and safely. With his other hand he was touching her hair. As if made of silk, his hand was sliding down her beautiful dark hair. Suddenly, he stopped the car on the side of the road once out of the town.

"Tina, should I call you Tina," he asked.

"Yes, of course, if you want to you can call me Tina."

"Tina, for a long time now I want to kiss you. I can only think about you and nothing else. I dream about kissing you. I want you to feel all my love for you."

"Igor, it is beautiful to hear you say that. It sounds like most relaxing music to my ears. You can see how the destiny connected us. I am extremely happy for that. In everything that happened to me lately, you were like a star in a dark night for me and I have been waiting for this day for a long time."

"Can I kiss you? For a long time now I want to kiss you. Please."

Igor took her face with his hands and pulled her gently towards himself. Ornella did not say anything, she just surrendered and offered her strawberry like lips. The time stopped in that moment and only the most beautiful melody could be heard surrounding them. Through their bodies beautiful warmth spread in waves. They kissed for a long time which seemed like an eternity.

"Igor, I'm not psychic but the whole time I felt that this will happen between us. I think from the first moment when I met you in the rain I felt it. Did you feel anything, tell me please?"

"I don't know really, only I was sure that I've never met a more beautiful woman in my life. I was not sure but secretly, I was hoping that one day you will be mine and no one else's."

"Oh Igor, I'm so happy for us. For a long time now I am planning to ask you something but I didn't know how you would accept it, now I will say it and you tell me what you think. I told you about everything, you know everything about me that I know. I'm sorry I wanted to ask you if you would mind travelling with me to Croatia. It would mean a lot to me if you would be able to come with me."

"Are you sure that you want that?" Igor was just somewhat surprised with her question.

"Absolutely, I'm totally sure. I want to go there, but I would like you to be with me because you understand everything I went through. I am afraid of meeting the land where I was born, I am afraid of my meeting with my father. That fear is driving me crazy and I'm worried I will not be able to do it."

"Tina, Me and you connected through our destinies from start, together we will go to the land where our ancestors come from. If this is your wish, for me it's a command. Don't worry at all, I will not let you go alone, I promise you."

“Thank you, Igor, you are a wonderful man,” said Ornella visibly very happy with his answer and feeling safe and secure in his presence.

Chapter VII

Northern Croatia, prison Lepoglava or *Lepoglava penitentiary*, the oldest prison in Croatia which was in operation since 1854. Thick iron bars made of steel in front of your eyes. The world looked incomplete when looking through them. The stench of prison was spreading for kilometres around and gave the sign that damned human souls lived there punished for eternity. But did they deserve to be punished is another story because after every war the victors write our history, and it is they who dictate the course of humanity's narrative. Yet, as the Latin adage "Historia Est Magistre Vitae" reminds us, history is meant to serve as a teacher for life.

The years were passing by very slowly there. They were dragging as if snails with their heavy houses on their back. How many exhausted faces, figures not defined, their skinny and hungry faces were not giving a sign of a life but some other strange contours that only from outside looked like human beings.

15 years ago, exactly, the member of this damned crew became Nikola Kovacevic, 33 years old rebel from the Northern Dalmatia region. He was a member of the paramilitary and as the Croatian side would describe them, the enemies of Croatia. He was sentenced by the military court in Croatia as a war criminal. Only Nikola knew that he was never that, but who would believe you when under the cruel club even the stone would start crying. His heart was tense, he tried to survive.

For all these years he has been living with only one hope in his wounded heart. Where are his loved ones? Years were passing, more slowly and more painfully but not once did anyone come looking for him. Slowly, he lights his cigarette and listens. The names of prisoners are echoing in the air. Nothing, again nothing.

All these years, he has been standing in the line and waiting for his name to be called, for someone to read his name on the list, to give him a letter. But it didn't happen. Not this time. Maybe he will have more luck next time. Maybe he needs to remain strong and wait and never give up hope. But that was easily said but not so easily done and accepted. The blind faith was wearing off after so many long years.

Hope, unexplained and not real still lived inside him. He was coming up with thousand reasons why his wife and children never wrote to him. He was thinking, as long as they are alive and healthy, nothing else is important. But what if his children forgot him? Where is his Vesna? He would close his eyes and return years backwards into the times when he was happy, in times that were left behind him, but he did not forget them. He would make these memories alive remembering and that was keeping him alive in all these difficult years.

Nikola was slowly turning into an old man. Weak grey hair and face full of wrinkles and scars. He was weak and very skinny. He was walking very slowly as if around his ankles were heavy chains. He would lift his hand quite slowly and his gaze was always distant. He would blink so slowly that someone next to him would think maybe he has fallen asleep while standing. He spoke very little, only when he had to. And that's how the days one after another were passing in sorrow and in suffering.

"Nikola, again no news from yours?" his friend from the neighbouring village, Stevan interrupted him whilst he was deep in his thoughts.

They were arrested together and served the sentence all those years. Stevan was of different nature, more talkative and a quite strong man. His wife and children were writing him regularly and he had hope.

"What do they say?" asked Nikola about Stevan's family as he received a letter.

"Nothing new, they say they are OK and they're healthy. You already know that my Marco married. My only wish is to leave this place alive and to see them again. I am hoping this hell we are living in will finish soon, we are very close to the end."

"Yes, you are right, but maybe these last moments are the hardest," said Nikola.

"I know, brother, I know but who knows, maybe this is what needed to happen. All these years were difficult for us like wounds on my body. If only I got shot that would be the best thing that could have happened to us to send us from this suffering. But even the death didn't want to take us," said Stevan.

"Do they mention anything about my family, maybe they heard something about them?" Nikola asked Stevan as he usually would after the letters were read.

"They said they didn't hear anything."

"How Stevan? How all these years they haven't heard anything about them? What could have happened? It is not possible that they couldn't get in touch with me. 15 years of this hell that I'm surviving here just so that I could see them one more time."

"Nikola, don't stress and worry too much. You have to worry for your health, you know you are weak," said Stevan whilst trying to support him.

"Stevan, all these years you never said that maybe they are not alive. Why didn't you at least once said something like that ever. I know that you suspect, you never ever said it," said Nikola while from his deep and tired eyes tears fell.

Stevan took a deep breath in.

"Don't, Nikola, I cannot say that because no one ever saw them. The hope still exists and I believe with all of my heart that they are all alive. We have to keep hoping."

"My Milan Should be 18 years old already grown-up man and my Igor 21. Tina should be 25 years old. They are already grown up people but I only remember them as children."

"It's OK, Nikola, calm down, it will pass, these last few months and then your soul will find its peace. You will get out of here and out of everything. Everything will end well, it has to end well. We did not throw stones on the God, we did not hurt anyone. We were unlucky. I always say this for hundredth time, if we went with Ilija, we would have managed to escape but we were stupid and listened to Uros and see where we are now. We are very naïve people as if we were kids playing the war games."

"Don't, Stevan, please don't, no one is at fault. Neither Ilija nor Uros knew what was the best to do. They only had more luck than us. My God, Stevan, you are talking about this like it was a month ago. When I only remember it feels like the time has not even moved. I wish we could return back into the past to fix our errors. That bloody morning I did not manage to get back into the village to tell Vesna and the kids to run. Only one thought is torturing me if they stayed at home and if they were killed there."

"Come on, Nikola, that is impossible. You know that somebody would let them know and they themselves would hear the shooting and they would know that they had to run."

"I don't know anything, Stevan, nothing at all because I ended up here, for all these years without knowing what happened to my loved ones. We were waiting for a pardon this whole time but it didn't happen. I thought the bastards will see that we did nothing wrong and that we never hurt a fly but still we got 15 years when they could not find anything against us."

"Hey, my Nikola, if there was one crime against you, trust me you would never leave this place but when they could not find anything against you and me, you got 15 years in this hell hole."

"So, Marko got married? How are they?" asked Nikola.

"They say it's not the best, but they are working hard for their bread. My wife is very sick. I'm scared she will die working as a slave on farms. I just hope she will wait for me. She's always writing, 'My Stevan, please stay alive just to see you one more time'. It's a bitter destiny and a heavy one. she said Marco married a good woman, she's hardworking and smart. I'm only praying for them to get along to respect each other that is all I wish for them. The dear God knows how much good I wish for them with my every breath."

"You see, Stevan, how are people melted away and disappeared. We spread all over the world. Our tradition and culture will be lost, our language will assimilate. You see how that all happens. Nothing is still."

"Yes, Nikola. What can we do there, nothing, absolutely nothing, let it be how it's going to be. I don't care about that anymore. I cannot change anything. If anybody asked me the end result would not be like this, I would find a peaceful solution for our people to live on their ancestral land but who asked me anything, Nikola. They told us to fight for freedom, but we lost the battle and our freedom. Otherwise, if we didn't, we wouldn't be in prison all these years."

"See, Stevan, how beautiful is this land. Look out there, at those green hills and meadows, like in a fairy tale. You see how beautiful it is? What I would give to be able to walk out there in that lovely nature and in freedom. I'm missing that space. Now, I'm like a bird in a cage and I'm missing my freedom.

"They took our freedom from us and I should be hating them from the bottom of my heart, but I don't hate them, I feel sorry for them. I cannot hate their children. My children, all these years live without any protection. But who knows maybe Vesna married again, maybe that's why they forgot about me? Oh God, I think I will go crazy from constantly wondering," said Nikola whilst holding his head with his both hands.

"Nikola Kovacevic," the prison guard called his name. Nikola as if coming out of a dream realised, he is called.

“The prison manager is asking for you. He needs you to come to his office immediately. Let’s go,” ordered the prison guard.

“Of course,” said Nikola slowly and followed the guard down the hall towards the office of the prison manager. The manager was sitting in a comfortable chair and looking through the window which was looking out into the back of the prison where prisoners would go out and walk to get daily exercise.

This person was looking at this every day. The lost human destinies walked around in circles in the prison from which they could not escape. The only place to look was up into the sky as if birds with broken wings who will never be able to fly.

Long ago, there was a lot of pride and dignity in those people. The prison director was asking himself where they got so much strength to survive this cruel place that, at times, he would start feeling scared of them. Their eyes were distant and when looking at him, he was able to feel as if they were lashing him with fire and might. As if they wanted their revenge for all the injustices committed against them. As if in their eyes he was able to see the fire of their revenge which made him unsafe and insecure around them.

But they were all around him, coming uninvited to his dreams as well. They never said anything, they only looked at him as if asking him silently why they were held in there. He felt guilty and his conscience was not in peace. Only he was aware how much he was afraid of those lost souls whose best years were spent behind the iron bars.

There were times when he thought it was harder for him then for them. “I have spent half of my life in this prison. I wonder what the hell would look like or maybe this is worse than hell.”

He was patiently waiting for his pension so that he can also get out of this prison. “Let someone young and new come and do this job, someone full of strength like I used to be once. Now, I do not have strength. This is not for me anymore, I’m too old for all of this and I cannot continue this power struggle,” he was thinking whilst walking from one wall to another.

“Nikola Kovacevic, how are you today?” he asked him as Nikola stepped into his office.

“Good,” said Nikola.

“Even today you are not in the good mood, Nikola. I’m looking at you through this window and I can see you are still distant in your thoughts, same like the day when they brought you in here. Soon you will leave this place. Are you happy because of that?"

"I'm too old now to understand the meaning of that. Maybe once upon a time I did know but that time has passed and I have started forgetting. It has been a very long time since I felt the meaning of that word."

"Don't be like that, Nikola. Not everything is black as it looks to you."

"Yes, you are right, all that is not black is grey," answered Nikola.

"Well fine, let me ask you something. Tell me have you heard anything from your family? Are they in contact with you?"

"No, they're not."

"And, what do you think about that, after all these years why is nobody contacting you, Nikola?" asked the prison director.

"Maybe they don't know that I am alive. Who knows where they are."

"How is it possible that only they never found out about you when all the others did. The bad news travels very fast across the borders."

"I don't know," answered Nikola briefly.

"Nikola, please listen to me carefully. It is not easy for me to talk to you about this but I decided that the time is right. You have been here for a long time and I know you from before this prison and this war that's now between us. We were neighbours, I know that you remember but times have changed and things stand out as they did, it is not your fault for what has happened to you and to my people. I know that."

"Why am I then in this prison if I am not guilty?"

"Nikola, you know why you are guilty, don't force me to tell you what you do not want to hear."

"It wasn't my choice to choose the people to belong to and the religion I was born into. I accepted all of that is mine because that is how our world turns around," said Nikola.

"Do you remember when we were young men in school? Both of us were in love with Vesna. She knew that and we knew that. I was crazy in love with her," said the director while breathing in deeply as if remembering those days and feelings. Nikola looked at him with an angry gaze full of fire still hiding in his heart.

"Don't look at me like that, please. A lot of time has passed since. But it is the truth, I did love her very much. I was dreaming that she will be only mine, but I did know that it will not be. Her black hair shiny like black pearls, her brown eyes and pale skin. I apologise, I know you do not want to listen to this. It just came to my mind unexpectedly.

"So, the reason why I called you in here. I have been thinking for a long time and decided to speak to you like I already told you. I have been asking around for a long time, very long, trying to find out about your family. I've been thinking if I should tell you and I did not find strength all these years. I thought no, I will not tell him what I found out but then again, I feel a duty to tell you. At the end I decided and that's why I asked you to come in here."

"Nikola, your wife and children were never registered with the Red Cross in Yugoslavia. I wanted to find out what happened to them. Unfortunately, they're all dead. They were killed that summer, 15 years ago. They were found dead. The soldiers from the United Nations found them. I think at that time your daughter was still alive but later, she died as well, I am not sure exactly how that happened. I am really sorry, Nikola. Please accept my condolences.

"Whilst I know that you will not believe me but really truly, I am so sorry for your loss, for your sorrow and grief. But I cannot change anything, believe me if I could, four of them would be alive now."

"Why didn't you tell me this earlier," asked Nikola as if frozen and in shock.

"I couldn't, please forgive me but I couldn't," he said while shaking his head from side to side.

"How were they killed?" asked Nikola still in shock and still standing in the same spot not moving not even a millimetre as if the news did not sink in as if this was not reality but a dream from which he will wake up shortly.

"I think they tried to rape Vesna; however, they did not because she killed a soldier with a knife. She was shot from the gun and the children as well. Nikola, I need you to be strong and survive this. I know that deep down you were expecting to hear this because it has been a long time and you never heard from them. I know that you were suspecting they were killed, otherwise they would have contacted you by now."

"I thought they were alive and healthy. I am crazy, Robert. You see what you did to us. Take now this little that is left, this life as well, Robert, please take it because everything else you already took from me. I am a destitute man, Robert, who except this painful life does not have anything else. I don't have anyone to live for. Take this heart from my chest, tear it out trust me you will do me a great favour and I will be grateful to you," said painfully Nikola begging for his life to end.

"Please don't say things like that. Please control yourself, it is not easy for me as well you know I am not guilty of anything."

"Yes, you are, you are guilty, you and others like you. Didn't the others like you killed them. It doesn't matter if it's not you personally, but you were all the same. You all think the same and you all hate so deeply. You cleansed your country from us and your century long dream came to fruition. But you know deep down, Robert, that this country belongs same to you and to us. This country is filled with blood of both of our peoples. Damn you forever. My children did nothing wrong to you, but you still killed them, worse than animals."

"Be careful what you are saying, Nikola, you are still in prison and you can be charged," warned him the director.

"Do you really think I care about any charges. I do not care at all. I could kill you with my hands now if I only wanted but I do not want to dirty my hands with you, Satan. I do not want to dirty my hands."

"For God's sake, I didn't kill your family," angrily yelled Robert.

"You would do the same, you are all the same. But I welcomed you all into my house. You ate food there, you drank wine there and I was proud. I didn't know that I was feeding and welcoming my own murderers for all those years. How stupid was I not knowing that you were my enemies and as soon as you have an opportunity, you will stab me with a knife in my back. How naive was I? I should have torn your heart out. If I could only have another chance, you would see how I would welcome you into my house."

"Please stop, Nikola, please stop. I am just an ordinary man, same like you. When evil enters human hearts, what did you think would happen. Everyone went with their own people when the war started. It was a civil war, Nikola, didn't we have two brothers on two sides of the conflict shooting on each other. Didn't we have situations where a son was shooting on his father. None of us are guilty. It was an evil time that came over us like a poison, maybe it was God's will."

"God has nothing to do with you, Robert. Your hands are bloody up to your elbows. I don't think that even your grandchildren will sleep in peace. Even they will be prosecuted by the souls of my children and of many more who like a seed were sown into this land. But you will never get rid of us because we are indestructible. We will rise again from the ashes and our souls will continue persecuting you. I promise you this is what's waiting for all of you, all of you whose hands are bloody from innocent victims."

"Guard, take him from here immediately and lock him up in his cell. I don't want to see him here again," ordered director loudly.

A dense darkness embraced this land. Always the same smell, the same feeling. Some were very scared of the dark. Others were talking about dead warriors marching through the nights. Their thoughts were not clear anymore and neither their hands nor their hearts. Not even their soul. Nothing was clean anymore. Only death existed, the death that wanted to swallow them in this dark night.

In the corner of his prison cell Nikola was squatting. He was holding his knees with his hands. He was looking into one spot. The darkness was swallowing him. His friend Stevan approached him and felt sorrow for him and wished he could help.

"What is with you, Nikola? You haven't eaten anything," noticed Stevan with worry in his voice. But Nikola did not respond and Stevan felt that even if he wanted to speak, he wouldn't be able to. He was silent like the earth beneath him which would talk instead of him if only possible. As if a stone, hard and old, he was like that and unable to speak.

"What happened, Nikola? You know you are weak and you need to eat regularly. Don't tell me you will give up now after 15 years. Are you going to let them see that and enjoy seeing you so weak? We still have some life to live but you, my friend, are behaving like the battle is lost and aapart of death, nothing else is waiting for us. For God's sakes you have not said a word since you returned back. Does this mean again I have to speak to myself? Come on, Nikola, speak to me please," Stevan tried his best to get him to talk. He sat on the ground next to him to be close.

"Please leave me," said Nikola with teary voice.

"Why are you crying, old man? What did you remember now? Do you think it's easier for me, it's not, it's not easy it is very hard. We can cry without stopping but we will not feel better. That's why I say stop crying and torturing yourself. I thought you were not able to cry anymore. I thought that your heart turned into a stone, unable to feel after all these years."

"Just leave me, I am not crying," said Nikola.

"OK, so you are not crying. Then why is your face wet?"

"They are falling on their own and I cannot stop them. Let them go."

"Nikola, are you not well again? You didn't eat, you know you have to eat regularly, please tell me what is happening," insisted his friend.

"I wish the death would take me this instant. It would be the best gift I could get today."

"Why are you saying that? The whole day you are not in a good mood. OK, I understand almost every day you are like this but today, it looks more serious and you are very quiet. Let's talk, my friend, maybe you will feel better. Why did our ex-friend and now the prison director called you today? What did he want from you?"

"It's all finished, Stevan, everything is finished—"

"What is finished? What are you talking about?"

"He told me everything today. The evil snake told me everything," said Nikola with anger in his voice.

"What about? What did that idiot say to make you feel this miserable?"

"They're all dead," said Nikola while looking deeply into his friends' eyes.

"Oh Nikola, my brother," said Stevan and embraced him. His eyes became heavy and tears fell down like rivers.

There was no more talk between them. Only silence and darkness. Only their cries could be heard as they were lifting from their chest and travelling through the darkness and disturbing the silence. They cried together embraced like that. Their hearts became gentler and softer and there were no words to be talked anymore, their tears were speaking instead of them now. And that in a nutshell is the philosophy of living and dying. That natural process of forever repeating in a cycle that never ends.

In all of that nature somewhere really you can find a human who is kneeling down with their hands placed together praying. That human is praying for the salvation of their soul and of the souls of their loved ones. In the nights when the dry winds blow from the mountains towards the sea, you can smell the hope and faith.

They never die because if they were going to die this path would be finished and not completed. Who knows how many more are going to be asking until when will this continue and when will this finish? It's interesting how some undefined power is pushing forward, these small human souls and their big hearts. It's leading them in one direction towards the goal.

Maybe the heart will become alive again once it touches the birth country. Maybe those grey rocks would remove the sorrow that lives in the heart. The wheel of fortune keeps turning faster and faster. Some of them are thrown out from it and they disappear but others, they continue on the path, sometimes clumsily falling down and getting up whereas the others are marching confidently forward.

That is the law. I wonder if our destiny could resist it? Could anyone really resist it? We don't know. Someone is writing the laws and choosing shepherds and herds. How long would this continue for we cannot know. Future, faith and hope remains. And where is love? If love disappears, if the heart turns into a stone what happens then?

Sometimes, the winds blow away from the sea. They bring the freshness of the sea and sorrow with them. That fragrant salty smell returns our soul back into the past and into the memories of our souls. The memories then become alive.

They dance a magical dance on the clouds which are chased by the wind. The clouds are not resisting, they follow the direction of the wind and they wander around. They are the real wanderers, the only free ones among us mere mortals. They do not have a homeland that they belong to but regardless they are very happy and at least to us, they look carefree. In front of them, limitless space without an end. But who knows, maybe they're scared of their freedom and infinity?

As famous Fjodor Dostojevski said once *What is hell? I maintain that it is the suffering of being unable to love.*

Chapter VIII

Australia is a vast country and a continent, entirely situated in the southern hemisphere between the Indian and the Pacific oceans. There is so much strength in it and she like a mother embraces her children keeping them removed far from danger among the southern seas. Although isolated and at the first sight lonely, she is nothing like that but a world on its own as if another planet in another Galaxy.

It is possible to love her with all your heart. Waves are breaking on her shores and taking away her sorrows. It took the white men many years to discover this gem hidden from their sight. Indigenous people probably wished this land stayed out of reach of the white men, but it was not to happen. The white men wanted this land for themselves, so they came and took it. Just like that, without asking anyone for permission.

Aboriginal and Torres Strait Islander people were not one united group but comprised of hundreds of groups that have their own distinct set of languages, histories and cultural traditions. This probably made it much easier for the white man to conquer the land without much resistance from the local people.

But the Aboriginal people are fascinating in many ways as if living on their own planet, so different from the one we got to know. One unique aspect of their culture was the Dreamtime, a term that describes unique stories and beliefs held by different Aboriginal groups. When you look more deeper into what dreamtime represents, you get the idea that the Aboriginal people imagine the world in a different way than the rest of us and they expressed it through their art.

In the central deserts of Australia, Jukurrpa is a traditional term used by some groups that describes what could possibly be similar to the religion as we know it and the laws for the people as we understand it. But there is more, in addition to religion and laws, they lay out the description of our reality that we live in. It is a very fascinating world which although distant from some of us, still connects deeply in our hearts us all as human beings.

So, this reality according to these Aboriginal people is a world created by our ancestor beings. The spirit of the ancestor beings remains in the country, in the animals and the places and the people of that country as an ongoing presence. How interesting? As if we are standing on the shoulders of our ancestors and although not here with us, their spirit is present and it's guiding us on our path through this challenging world.

The blue sea was connecting with the blue sky into one horizontal line. Exactly there amongst those cool colours resides peace and prosperity. They live together and believe in each other's existence. Happiness lives there as well but not everyone is able to find it. As if able to see into the past for a moment seeing big and powerful ships coming towards the shores.

The one standing and looking would feel what kind of feelings I wonder. Would that person feel fear of the unknown, danger from such a powerful big ship or maybe excitement that this meeting would bring new possibilities. Now in present times, we know how it played out when an advanced civilisation landed on these shores and transformed this land forever. The beauty of the land was still preserved and visible all around you.

But even in this vast and beautiful country pain was felt by those who lived here for centuries. If you look deep down under the surface, you will still feel the pain around now carried by their descendants. This isolated jewel in the southern sea was conquered not long ago by us, people from the north. Did we spread our war and struggles into this ancient land bringing with us modern weapons and ways only acceptable to us?

Ornella was watching the waves. They were enormous and very powerful. One after another they were breaking off the stones into thousands smaller waves that were disappearing into the greatness of the sea. The wind ruffled her hair and caressed her face. She would close her eyes in that moment and enjoy in her peace. Igor approached her and hugged her gently kissing her face. She smiled back with her eyes still closed, enjoying in his subtle touch.

"What are you thinking about beautiful woman?" he asked her while kissing her face.

"Nothing really. I'm watching waves and how they're breaking off the stones. The waves are like our lives going in circles. Look there! One wave is climbing up so high and storming towards the stones and behind him, another one is already coming again and rushing to put an end on their short existence. Who is chasing them, it's the wind, of course. The wind is their force pushing them forward. They whole existence and strength depends on wind. The waves probably respect the wind for that, they are grateful for their lives and they adore the wind like a God."

"Eh my Angel, what are you thinking about? It is that way because it has to be that way. It is like happiness that lasts forever or like love that lasts even after death separates them."

"Do you think love lasts even after the death?" she asked him surprisingly turning towards him to see his answer.

"Yes, of course, it lasts after death if it is the real true powerful love."

"It sounds so beautiful hearing you say that. Can love then disappear in some people? How can the ones that possess love be able to kill?"

"I don't think that everyone possesses love, only those rare ones whose eyes are looking innocently and, on whose paths, there are no fogs. Only they have the power to feel the richness of that feeling. I do believe that hearts full of hate and locked away into the maze of disappointment exists. Even still alive, these are like cursed from God and lost souls."

"That sounds so sad. You know I have been thinking about my father. I am scared of that meeting. What if his heart turned into a stone full of hatred and pain? I'm really scared of my meeting with him. I have a feeling that sometimes in my dreams I am walking through the corridors of a prison and I see him and he looks like an old man hunch down but not old from the old age but old from something else.

"He looks at me, but he looks through me and he doesn't see me. I am calling him, but he doesn't turn around and he leaves. Just once he told me leave me so I can die and don't come to me anymore. I said I'm not here to hurt you, but he answered why are you then coming to me, leave me, I am sick.

"Igor, I am worried about this why is this happening to me now. What if he's really sick or what if he dies before getting out. I am really scared. But I need to see him I need to see him as soon as possible."

"Don't be scared, you know you need to prioritise your health after everything that happened. Don't scare me again, please don't."

"OK, so how was today at your work?"

"Same as always. We have problems with some drug dealers. I'm hoping soon we will be dismantling them and arresting few in the process. Maybe you will not see me or hear from me in a few days until that's all finished."

"What do you mean?" she asked with a surprise in her voice.

"It's nothing really unusual but we need to do the job well. You don't have any reason for worry. I'm a policeman and my job is like that as you already know."

"I don't really like that, to be honest."

"Well, it's like that whether you like it or not. But let's forget that, I need to ask you something," he said trying to change the topic.

The sun was melting into the horizon as it was falling down and the dusk was enclosing on them together with the sea as their witness whilst they were in each other's embrace.

"OK, of course, you can ask," Ornella curiously responded.

"Well—I'm not sure how to start—"

"Come on—come on—you have to tell me now—you can't keep me in suspense," said Ornella still excited.

"Tina, will you marry me and spend the rest of your days with me as my wife, please," said Igor whilst taking a small red box from his pocket.

A beautiful shiny ring was in the box. He took it out and put it on her finger. Her eyes were filled with tears but happy tears this time. She looked at the ring on her finger and smiled contently. Igor was observing like watching from a side while she was not saying anything. She was gentle and sweet, like a little girl enjoying in her moment. A very special moment indeed.

"Answer me, my love, why are you silent?" asked Igor but still no word came from her.

"Why are you crying now, please don't cry," he noticed her tears.

"I will marry you. Of course, you know I will," she said and fell into his embrace. He responded the same, embracing her tightly and passionately. Igor smiled with content, thinking to himself how good the life could be if there could be more beautiful moments like these. This special moment in their lives will be remembered forever.

"Igor, I don't know much about you, but I feel I have known you forever. Do you think we are hurrying things?"

"We are, I agree but like you said, we already know each other for eternity. I can't imagine my life without you and I want to show you that I don't need to be dating you for years before feeling ready for the next step. I know now what I want and that is to share this life with you. I'm afraid to say it but I have this feeling inside me that I've already wanted to be with you and something didn't let us in some other life, I'm not sure, it doesn't sound right to say it like this, but I do not want to lose you."

"You will not lose me. I haven't been in a similar situation before; I haven't been in relationships and maybe, I don't know how to behave or what to expect. This is all very new for me and to be honest until I met you, I was completely fine to go through this life alone.

"Now that I know you, I cannot imagine life without you. I want a life where we are together and we have family, our children, I want everything with you. And like you, I also feel deep down there is fear that we will not be able to have it, that something will stop us. Maybe our souls recognised each other or maybe it's because your name was familiar to me because my own brother was called Igor, I don't know, I don't have any answers."

"We don't need to be sure and know everything. We just need to be together and slowly things will come into its place and we will find the place in this world. Love can conquer all. Like you, I also don't have much experience in relationships. There was no one, tempting my attention and with work being so busy, I didn't really pay too much attention to it. You walked into my life suddenly, but my life has not been the same after that day and you know it. It is almost like there was no life before you but only life from that moment onwards," said Igor.

"Are we ready to go home," Igor asked.

"Not yet, let's walk on the beach to feel the silky sand under our feet," suggested Ornella and he accepted.

"You know tomorrow I will not see you because of work but the day after tomorrow, we will meet for sure."

"Promise, you will be in contact," requested Ornella.

"Of course, like always, I will. You don't worry about anything, just focus on yourself and no stress. After this job, I am planning to take leave from work and then off we go to Croatia. What do you think? It's a good idea? I will be able to help with the language," he suggested pulling her towards himself and kissing on her forehead.

"It's a deal, boss," she answered contently.

Ornella was walking home in a hurry. She wanted to share her happiness with her loved ones.

"Mum—Dad—" she called from outside.

"What happened? Why are you so happy?" asked her father Steve walking in rush towards her.

"I am so happy. Today's my happiest day ever," Ornella said and showed her hand and the ring on her finger. Her parents were looking surprised.

"What Happened?" her father kept asking.

"Igor proposed to me. He wants me to marry him," she said showing the ring on her finger to both of them. Rosie quickly embraced her and Steve joined them.

"It is a wonderful news, my daughter, a wonderful news at last. Congratulations to both of you darling. You really pleasantly surprised us," said her mother, Rosie.

"Ornella, where did this come from so quickly, isn't it rushed a bit. Why are you in a hurry?" asked her father.

"Maybe you are right, Dad, maybe we are in a hurry, but I don't know. It feels right and I feel ready. Igor is a wonderful man; he is kind and good. I am deeply in love with him and I thought I could never fall in love, I thought that was not for me but somehow, he showed me the way and with him, I feel safe. I think everything will work out. Please don't worry about us."

"Steve, don't say that. They are young and full of energy for life. Have you already forgotten how we were?" reminded him Rosie.

"I Understand everything you say, but I still feel this is rushed. You don't know each other for a long time, my child. The marriage is something more serious than being in love. It is not like a relationship of falling in love, it is more complicated than that. I feel like you are back to your teenage years, making rushed decisions.

"You really surprised me and I did not expect this from you. Marriage is a complex union where many compromises need to be made. You have to be ready for that in advance. Those quick relationships break when first problem arises and then what will happen. You can be hurt and heartbroken. You needed to give this a bit more thought, my darling."

"But, Dad—I am no longer a small child. I am 25 years old and I know what I want from life. Please try to understand me. I have grown up but maybe you haven't noticed. I agree with you when you say that everything was rushed and way too fast. I do agree with you. But we did not feel the time pass nor did we feel that this was rushed. Love is like this. It burns like fire. Try to remember when you were young, maybe then you would be able to understand us," said Ornella smiling.

"Congratulations, my dear, you know I wish you all the happiness in this world. I have to admit I have been dreading this time when I will lose you. You know how much you mean to us. I have become old and I'm not so understanding like we used to be. We only think about ourselves, we are very selfish. I know you will understand me but maybe this is good news, maybe the time has come for me to become a grandfather.

"You see how time flies. It feels like yesterday when you came to us. You were the most beautiful, sweet girl, restless and fast, full of energy and life. Oh my God, how this time is flying by and we are getting older from day to day."

"Don't worry and don't talk like that, you will make me sad. This is a happy moment. I wish you can feel at least one drop of this happiness that now is burning inside me. It's like a strength that's moving me it is love. Love for you and love for Igor—"

Her eyes suddenly became teary and a cloud of sadness appeared around her. She stopped talking. Her parents understood where her thoughts were flying in those moments. She wanted to return back. But they were dreading that day. 'What if she stays there forever?'

This was a possibility worrying them the most. It was like a knife tearing their hearts in pieces and with every day, they were fearing that they are losing her and that she was less theirs as days were passing by. And now this sudden ring and proposal, made them feel the fear even stronger.

Ornella woke up very early in the morning. The day was fresh, a little bit cold and the wind was quite strong. She opened the window to breathe in the fresh air. Ornella continued doing this since being in the hospital where every day she would start like this. Wide open window in early mornings, allowing fresh and cold air to fill her lungs and awaken every cell in her body.

The weather had always been a significant factor in her life, and on windy days like this, it seemed to stir up storms inside her that manifested first in her behaviour. She felt a strong urge to be alone, and her once lively and vibrant voice would become gentle and sensitive. She quickly dressed up, running outside to escape the turmoil brewing within.

Mornings were always special to her. It was the time when she felt the closest to nature, and everything around her seemed to radiate with beauty and peace. The only sound was the gentle rustling of the leaves as the wind blew through the trees. She began walking down the garden path in front of her family home, lost in memories of her childhood. The curly parts of the garden, the paths that melted into each other – they were all still there, just as she remembered.

The sky above her was clear, devoid of clouds. Despite the tranquil surroundings, a familiar nervous feeling crept into her body, and she didn't like it. Time seemed to slow down, just when she wished it would speed up. She longed to close her eyes and for time to rush by, so that she could move on from this waiting game. But the days felt like years, and her thoughts drifted further away.

"How is that poor man surviving in that prison for all these years when I out in freedom have difficulty waiting for that day, When I will return back to my homeland. I think his days must be heavy like chains around his feet. What do the nights look like, my God, how does he stand the long nights?

"Oh dear, all mighty God, I pray to you now in this moment because your power is so great it is limitless, please give strength to my father. Please gift him strength which I'm sure he does not have left anymore. Please dear God, gift him clear and sane mind so that he does not give up. I would hug him tightly now if I was able to, please send me to him in his dreams and let us embrace one another.

"How did he deserve to suffer so much and to lose everything? Where did the punishment come from, oh dear and merciful God. You punished him and me to suffer enormous pains. The road we need to walk is difficult.

"My memory returned so clearly. The land feels distant and in fog but it is again alive in me. I am running to meet some people, they are soldiers in uniforms. One of them takes me into his embrace and he kisses me. He says I'm beautiful and that I need to be good. My mother is asking me to come into the house, she's yelling about something. I am leaving but they are continuing on the rugged path. Under their military boots the earth is trembling. I am watching their legs how they are marching in synchronicity.

"The weather is hot, it is summer. The sun's warmth is reflecting on them and down their unshaved faces sweat is falling. I am looking at them, for a long time I am looking. I asked myself where they were going and who will they be shooting at with those big guns.

"My mother she's yelling again she wants me to go into the house. I asked her if my father is there and I'm showing with my hand into the distance where the soldiers were. She says no and she takes me by hand into the house. Even today, I asked myself who were those people and where were they going. Did they die in the war or were they arrested like my father? Maybe, they're alive and now only in stories talk about their days from their youth. Who will know the answer?"

"Ornella, where are you going?" asked her mother.

"I will go for a drive towards the city. I feel like moving and might as well," said Ornella quickly entering into her car.

"Did you hear from Igor? Did something happen?" asked her mother concerned.

"Don't worry, Mum, everything is fine. We didn't get a chance to fight because we didn't even see each other," said Ornella casually calming her mother not to worry too much.

The car was on a wide road going fast. Mid-day was soon. The air in the car felt old so she opened her window to get new and fresh air. In the mirror, she noticed herself looking kind of worried and serious. Igor was not contacting her since he proposed to her and it started to worry her somewhat, only she would not admit to herself. In her mind she was looking for excuses, why he was not able to find even few minutes just to call her quickly and tell her that he was fine. As time was passing, she felt upset with Igor. Why keep her waiting and in suspense? What was the reason for this?

After a long drive Ornella arrived to Igor's workplace. There was a bit of uncomfortable feeling inside her and she wanted to reassure herself all was good.

"Good day, sir, I am looking for Igor Savic, your colleague," asked Ornella confidently.

"What are you to him, Ms?" asked the police officer.

"I am his fiancé," said Ornella feeling a bit uncomfortable with all the questions. The police officer looked at her with frown on his face as if suspicious.

"Come with me, Ms," he ordered briefly and decisively.

They were walking down the long narrow corridor and Ornella started feeling quite uncomfortable trying to predict Igor's reaction when he sees her. Maybe she needed to wait longer, it has only been two days. He has busy at work and she should have waited for him to call her instead of barging like this uninvited.

She was trying to convince herself to accept the fact that Igor is a police officer and that was his profession and his career that he chose. She needed to respect that and give him space. Who knows what kind of issues can come up. Longer she was going down corridor, more she was feeling uncomfortable about her decision to come to look for him.

Feeling of nervousness was in her and the whole atmosphere was somehow stressful. They arrived to the end of the corridor where the other police officer stopped and asked her to prove her identity by showing her identity card. She showed drivers licence and the police officer looked at it and at her, trying to determine that it was the same person.

"Ornella Moon?" the officer read her name from the card. "Please wait here a little bit."

"OK, no problems, I will wait."

"Please come in here, Ms Moon."

She looked curiously around her and noticed a detective room. Once inside the room, a sergeant greeted her.

"I am Sargent Sancez," the officer introduced himself. "I am Igor's boss as we would say."

"Mr Sancez, I'm really sorry I did not have any intention to disturb you. I was hoping to find my fiancé Igor here. Is he not here?" asked Ornella now even more confused not understanding what was the big deal and why take her to this room.

"Igor Savic is your fiancé? I did not know. Igor is a good lad. I think he is an excellent man and police officer. I think you are very lucky young lady."

"Thank you, Sargent."

"So, you are here to see him. Let's get straight on to the matter," said the Sargent seriously.

"Igor had a job with drug dealers. We found a warehouse from where they were moving the drugs. The information received was wrong, one of the men responded badly when he saw the police and started fighting with us. Igor thought that he was going to shoot but the man did not have any weapons on him. Igor shot him, as he claims in self-defence. It was later determined that man had no weapons on him. Unfortunately, the man has died later in the hospital.

He was 42 years old and this morning, we had to inform his wife and kids. Igor killed an innocent man."

"Oh my god, this is too much to take. Where is he now? How is he?" asked Ornella still in shock.

"I will get a police officer to take you to him. I'm hoping everything will end well for him because he acted as trained."

"This is terrible, this is too much for me to bear. I can't even imagine how is Igor feeling."

"Our work is like this, miss. You never know what waits for you. The danger is always around the corner."

Young police officer took her up the steps and then through another long corridor. After the terrible news that she received only minutes ago, she felt terrible. She kept following the officer in front of her but it felt that the building was cycling around making her dizzy as if going through maze.

She was not sure where she was, nor where she was going to. How did this happen to him? How did he let this happen? Too many questions but no answers. The young police officer showed her with his hand the door. Ornella entered the room and noticed Igor sitting deep in the corner. No one was saying one word, they were just staying like that in silence. There was nobody else in the room. Ornella approached him slowly and carefully.

"Igor, will you not look at me?" she whispered insecurely. Slowly she approached him, coming very close to him, caressing his hair with her hand. Igor was sitting in silence and as if crying, his face was swollen, maybe from lack of sleep. His body looked exhausted and tired, it was visible from the way he was sitting and looking like.

"Igor, what happened to you? Please talk to me."

"I don't know—I really don't know what happened. The only thing I know is that I will go crazy in this room. I feel so powerless. Damn it—I killed a man—an innocent man. Oh God—How could I do that? How could I make such a mistake?" he spoke disconnected and with worry on his face.

"It is not your fault," she interrupted him after seeing and feeling his pain.

"Whose fault is it then? Who is at fault you tell me please, if it's not me who is?" Igor responded in frustration.

"I understand it is hard for you. But it is hard to listen that you are blaming yourself. I cannot listen to that because I know you are not at fault. This could have happened to anyone."

"But it didn't happen to anyone, it happened to me. But why me? I didn't want it to be me. Why did I kill an innocent man, he did not deserve to die for nothing?" His eyes were burning with fire, inside his chest only emptiness and sadness. A burden of the accident was visible. What if it was just a bad dream and someone was going to wake him up and this will all be forgotten very quickly.

"Who informed you about it?" Igor asked Ornella.

"You never called me like you promised, so I came to your work to see what you were doing. I didn't even know what nightmare you are living here. I'm so sorry this has happened to you. What will happen now? Do you know what to expect?"

"How can I think about anything else, but about the man whose life I took away. I feel useless, how could I even think that he had a gun. I thought he had a gun, but he didn't have anything, he was just an ordinary man working in a warehouse."

"It's OK, Igor, don't torture yourself with these memories," Ornella hugged him tightly letting him know she was there supporting him and he was not alone.

"I am so desperate, powerless. If I was able to find enough strength to end this suffering, I would do it, I would stop living. I know exactly what is waiting for me ahead and I'm not ready to face it," his cry was loud and he found shelter in her embrace.

Ornella felt the heaviness of the moment and the pain he was feeling. She was not able to lessen his load, she was only able to be there for him in that moment. She was only able to hug him tightly and wish for this moment to pass as fast as possible. He was crying for a long time and holding onto her. She cried for him as well, maybe more than him.

"Please don't cry. I don't want something happening to you after everything you went through."

Igor although in an extremely difficult situation was still thinking about her, worried about her health.

"Igor, if you wish my father can be your lawyer, just tell me if you want that, just in case the police have to prosecute the case. This all happened so quickly and I'm trying to think what the best course of action is."

"Don't worry, police will provide their lawyers and everything should be fine because I was on duty. I am not afraid of law or sentence that I might get. I am afraid of myself and how will I live with this going forward. Please I don't want to see you worry this much. You should go now and leave me alone. I think I need to be alone," he said moving away from her towards the window.

"I will come back tomorrow," she said and kissed him on his cheek and started walking towards the door. Igor turned around looking at her. She turned to look back and they eyes locked in one. She returned back into his embrace.

"I love you, Igor, I love you so much."

"I love you too, very much, more than you can even imagine. Don't worry about me, everything will be well. I will get out of here I promise. I don't need any help you will see everything will be fine."

"Igor, you are not guilty of anything, please don't continue blaming yourself, it was an accident. I believe in you, you are a good person."

"How can you believe in someone who made such a stupid mistake? You should be embarrassed of me; you should not look at me or speak to me. You should forget me."

"Stop, I don't want to hear that. I believe in you. What happened to you could have happened to anybody else. It was an accident at work. Please be strong and get help. I know you are brave and courageous and you will survive this, but I also know it will not be easy. Be strong for both of us."

Ornella left the police station and walked out. So many questions in her head but no answers. How will she cope with this and how will Igor? Leaving him there on his own was not easy but he reassured her he would be fine and police will support him. A small doubt in her heart was burning. What if Igor does not survive this, what if what happened changes him forever? Why him and why now? No answers were coming to her, only doubts and questions. It's best to let things just go and hope for the best, she thought.

Chapter IX

"That day has arrived, Nikola Kovcevic. You will be free very soon. When I think about it, well, it went fast, don't you agree?" asked the prison director with menace in his voice.

Nikola listened but did not respond. Still like a prisoner used to listen and take orders as if still serving his sentence as if still he had many more years to serve.

"How do you feel now? Relax, please," continued the director.

"I feel like a bird leaving the cage but with broken wings, Mister. Did you ever think I would be addressing you as Mister," responded Nikola looking sharply at the director with rage and anger in his eyes. He wanted revenge to satisfy his pain. The fire was still burning inside him but he did not have much strength. The long 15 years behind the iron bars took from him everything he had and now he was weak.

"Let it go, Nikola, we already talked about it last time. A lot of time has passed and time heals the wounds. Now, you see what kind of mistake you made when you decided to go to war against this country. You were found guilty and you served the sentence. Unfortunately, your commanders are walking freely in Serbia but here you were serving the sentence. I hope you learned your lesson.

"But, you are weak now, no one will be able to have any use of you. You don't have anybody, you lost everything. The war took everyone from you but you are still upset, same like that day when they brought you here. How many more years do you need to spend in this prison to learn your lesson. Don't you see that all these years you lived in denial of the truth? Do you even understand what's happened here? I think you understand, Nikola, but you are pretending not to understand. You are full of hatred—"

"Are you full of love, Robert?" Nikola interrupted him whilst talking and asked the question with sarcasm in his voice. The director did not like that and became visibly upset and nervous.

"I will ask you to pay attention to your words. I know that you are disappointed but don't forget, you only have yourself to blame. Don't be upset with one just and righteous people. We are not at fault. You got what you deserved and now, it's finished, it's too late for everything. Like I said, you got what you asked for. But let's put that aside let me ask you where are you going now?"

"I will go back home," Nikola said.

"What home, Nikola? Are you listening to yourself. The house is destroyed 15 years ago. Don't act like you don't understand. I am asking you seriously."

"I am answering to you seriously. I will go back home. I was scared I would die here. My wish is to finish this difficult life there where I came into this world. I wish to die on that land that was feeding me, that land for which I went to war and fought for all these years. For that land I spent full 15 years in this prison.

"Where should I go now if not there? Whom else should I return if not to that red dry land and painful memories. Except it and this useless life, I do not have anything else left. I lost everything that a man can lose, I cannot lose more, this is the end. I will go back there. Maybe it's the best because that is the only place I belong to."

"Oh no—no—Nikola. You do not belong there. Who will be waiting for you there? What are you going to find there?" asked the director.

"The most beautiful memories are waiting for me there which gave me strength to survive my sentence. The graves of my parents are there and my wife and children. I want to visit their last resting place and cry for them. I want to bring a flower on their graves because I know no one visited them all these years. I will do that; it is my last mission."

"You will return to graves, Nikola, are you listening to yourself, for god's sake. It is better for you to go to Zagreb to a nursing home to wait for your death there because you will die soon, you don't have much strength left, you are exhausted and ill."

"Am I free now?" asked Nikola.

"Yes, you are," answered the director.

"If it is like that, I will go where I want and not where you order me to. And please don't be concerned for me that much, I had enough of your concern for the past 15 years."

"Nikola, I know for a long time what happened to Vesna and kids. If I told you then you would not be here now, you would not be able to see the end of prison sentence."

"Thank you for your concern, Robert."

"Don't thank me, please. You know deep down I respected you and did not forget the days from our youth. You were not lucky, Nikola and truly, I am sorry for everything that happened to you, you did not deserve it. I know you will not believe me, but I tried many times to reduce your sentence, but I wasn't able to, I just wasn't.

"Do you think I believe you killed those people? No way, Nikola, you would not be able to harm an ant, but you never gave me a chance to help you, you did not want to listen, you were too proud and hurt. I am not saying this because I am scared of your curse and your sharp words. I am telling you what I feel. This is the truth, but it is OK, you don't need to believe me.

"Anyway, it is not important now, it is too late to say anything, it is too late for it. The time has passed since and new people were born into this world, some of them don't even want to hear about our bloody war. They don't understand the sacrifices and victims who paid with their lives.

"Now I understand how cruel and senseless this life can be. This is all a big nonsense but no worries. I wish for you to find your path and I am not looking for an apology for all those heavy words you said to me. Who knows if I was in your shoes what words I would tell you. I want you to know that everything I said come from my heart and that I truly think this. Good luck, Nikola," said director and extended his hand for a handshake.

Nikola looked at his hand for a few moments but at the end, he took his hand and shook it. Director's eyes filled with tears in that moment and he remembered their youth and happier times. Nikola noticed this and responded in kind with an awkward smile.

He felt he understood what the director was talking about as he also shared similar feelings. So much hatred and love at the same time. Who was the one that managed to make enemies of them? It was too late to fill the gap between them, too much happened, there was no way back only forward. They will never be friends again, they can only dwell on past memories prior to the war which divided them forever.

"Thank you, Robert," said Nikola, with a quiet voice.

Robert quickly removed the tears from his face with his hands and turned his back towards the window looking down into the prison. Nikola left the office. The prison guard followed him to his cell where he collected few little things that he accumulated over the years. He imagined this day differently and now that it was here, he didn't feel much, it felt like any other day. He thought when this day arrives, he will get out of this place full of strength to go and look for his family but now, things were different.

Now that he was out, his loved ones were waiting for him but under the ground laying there in cold earth for the past 15 years. Stevan left last month and apart of him he spoke to no one so leaving will be easy. Once Stevan left, there was no one there to talk to him, only his thoughts and him.

"Where did my 15 years go? My God, where did my life go? I had so many plans, what to do when I get out of here. So many plans with my wife and kids but now, there is nothing ahead of me. Who did I go to the war for? Eh my cursed homeland, your soil is full of blood and you will never live in happiness again. Where brother shoots on his brother, there is no happiness left. In my memory so many pictures when there was enough space for everyone and when we managed to live in harmony with one another.

"As if the good lives we lived and prosperity we achieved turned into boredom and we needed to fight. You are cursed my beloved homeland; I know you are because every generation has to fight wars on your soil. You don't like peace. You look so beautiful but underneath your beauty, hell fires are burning. What was I supposed to do? Resist the war but how? At the time, I thought I have to go or risk being considered a traitor, I had to protect my children. God is my witness, I have not killed anyone but for someone else's crime, I served the sentence. I stayed behind the bars instead of another bastard.

"Is this how life is? You can be cheated and used and the real monsters are outside walking in freedom. What I am to think after that? Am I to think that I deserved this life to turn like this? Did God decide to punish me like this but for what reason. I believed in God and followed him but as a reward I received a sentence to serve others' crimes.

"If only my children were alive, I would not complain, dear God, not one word I said all these years, begging you to protect them while I was away so that I can see them once more in this life. But it did not work, they were not protected by you, my Lord, they were abandoned by you and by me."

Nikola was walking towards the exit of the prison and while walking out, he was in deep conversation with his own thoughts.

Tall younger looking prison guard took him towards the gate. Nikola in him saw his Igor, now if he survived he would be like this young man, in his best youth.

"Nikola Kovacevic, please take this letter. I received an order to give you this letter when you leave this place."

"What is this letter?" asked Nikola surprised.

"I do not know. I was not told what it's about, only to give it to you which I have now done. That is all I can say," said the young prison guard signalling to Nikola he was not told anything about it.

Nikola took the envelope turning around. Then suddenly he stood there looking at the prison one more time. Up on the window of the tall building he could see Robert's shadow. Like always, he was staying there next to the window looking at the yard. Nikola opened the envelope and saw several large notes in Croatian money. He looked back towards the window where Robert was still standing. Nikola took a deep breath in and closed the envelope. In that moment he was not sure what he was feeling, confusing thoughts in his head. He left the prison followed by Robert's eyes as he was leaving.

As he walk out of the prison he did not turn anymore. Although he wanted to, he didn't. As if something was pulling him away to turn and look back at the place where he spent the last 15 years but he resisted and did not turn. Tears started falling down his tired face and blinded him.

He felt the sadness again and hatred in his heart. He could feel his lower lip shaking and his eyes full of tears were looking around very quickly. To keep living he didn't have much strength but to die he could not. So where then to go after everything? His weak legs were lifting up from the ground heavily.

His breath was heavy and fast, and, in his hands, he was holding the envelope like a cramp. For years he was imagining the moment when he was going to be given an envelope. All these years he was dreaming about reading the letter written by a well-known handwriting. But years passed and the letter never arrived. The hope would disappear sometimes but then come back again. With years, the hope was becoming smaller because deep down in his soul he did expect the worst.

From nowhere some strange strength entered his body and he suddenly felt the freedom. From all his strength he roared, the sound of his voice echoed back to him from the distance. This moment he lived for all these years. The man is like a bird, he has to be free to fly through the life.

Nikola was aware of his situation, he was no longer that bird that could fly, he was a wounded bird with broken wings and powerless but still free. His face was dark from scars and old age. He looked like an old man tired of life although he was still young by age, only 48 years old. The cruel life exhausted him and gave him this elderly look to carry around like a proof of his burden.

His body was trembling but deep down, there was a tiny fire still burning inside his chest. As he was moved away from the prison, the fire was becoming greater.

"Once I step onto my country, the fire will return back," Nikola was thinking deep down focusing with all his strength on his next destination, on his return back home to his village, to his ancestral country.

Chapter X

Ornella was walking up and down the garden nervously. Different thoughts were wandering inside her head and she was not able to focus. She was not able to calm down. As if some kind of confusion was ruling in her human body and she was feeling its reactions to how she was feeling. She felt completely powerless, not being able to do anything that would change the outcome. Still attempting to understand the situation logically from a bigger picture perspective and connecting the dots but it wasn't working.

The sergeant promised her last time when she spoke to him that he would do everything that was in his power to protect Igor. He went into details about his plan how to handle the complex situation. He also convinced her to believe that everything will turn out OK in the end. Igor should be able to get out of this mess and he will need to continue living only with his own guilt of participating in the incident and causing someone's death.

Ornella was focusing more on the end result, not so much on Igor's thoughts. She understood it was a long road ahead of him and maybe in time, he will accept his fate. All of her intentions were focused on seeing Igor free. Was that the justice? She could not answer because she was being led by her subjective feelings and her love for Igor. His fearful and disappointed face was still in front of her eyes. She got the feeling that he processed the things and was fine, but still, his eyes were full of rage and disappointment in himself.

He spoke very little and appeared worried and distant. Ornella clearly remembered what he looked like when he talked about the tragic incident. She was playing that picture in her head for thousand times.

"Did they feel like that? Those criminals who decided on that warm day to kill my mother and two brothers," she asked loudly and remembered how she was feeling thirst on her dry lips.

"Yes, same, like now I was really thirsty that day, I was extremely thirsty but not just me, all of us were thirsty. I went to look for water. Yes, that's why I avoided the enemies bullets. Now I remember, that's how it was. I remember their faces, they were dirty and cold. The eyes were red, their eyes full of blood were chasing me in my dreams. They looked like damned animals, oh vampires who were looking for warm blood of their victims."

"Ornella, darling, are you talking to yourself," Steve interrupted her.

"Oh, Dad, yes, you are right I was talking with my own thoughts."

"What is bothering you, my dear," asked Steve approaching her and giving her a hug.

"Well, it's not important I guess."

"OK, can I ask you, my darling, how are you? We see you rarely nowadays. As if you are trying to avoid us, as if you were hiding from us. Sorry for coming to this conclusion but I really think like that and your mum agrees with me. Why are you always on your own and you look very disappointed and quiet?"

"Oh—Dad—I am sorry—I apologise for constantly worrying you but I feel terrible, truly I feel very bad and I don't want to worry you with this stuff. Exactly now when you came I was thinking about the people who killed my mother and brothers. Did they feel guilty after the crime they committed? What do you think, Dad?" she asked curiously.

"Well—I don't know—I'm guessing they didn't feel guilty. For them, maybe it was something easy to do. But then again, who knows, my daughter, I don't know what to think. On one hand, I think who knows how many people they killed. Probably your mum and brothers were not the only ones. They could have been professional killers, soldiers fighting in a cruel and bloody war. Yes—I would not be surprised if they killed many innocent people, otherwise they wouldn't shoot at civilians. It is impossible to know, my dear, I am just guessing."

"Do you think they are treating him badly in the prison?"

"Who?" asked Steve

"My father. He is in prison for 15 years. I think it is very long and that he had many traumas to survive. It's a very long time to spend behind the bars. Do you think that my father is also a killer, that he was like those soldiers I witnessed killing my mother and brothers, that he also killed like that, children and women? What do you think about that, Dad?" asked Ornella with visible concern on her face.

"Well, again, my darling, I don't know, you will have to ask him. Maybe he did or maybe he didn't."

"Why would he be sentenced as a war criminal to spend 15 years if he never killed anyone, if he never did anything wrong?"

"Ornella, you need to understand one thing. The winners always write the history. Your father was on the defeated side, on the side that lost the war and what can you expect after that. They could have found many things to pin on him if they wanted to. I don't know your father but I want to believe that your father was not a war criminal and I think you should not believe in that as well.

"You have to free yourself from that thought otherwise it will be difficult for you, my darling. Listen to me, Ornella, you always need to have a dose of optimism in your heart, try to understand certain actions from a bigger picture perspective. You will never know for sure why did they react the way they did but often from my life experience, what I have seen is the truth sometimes is not what it seems it is."

"Oh, my god, I'm asking myself how Igor is feeling right now. Is he better?" asked Ornella and took a deep breath in.

"Well, what happened to Igor, is he sick?" asked her father surprisingly.

"Oh—no—no—he is not," answered Ornella realising she was thinking loud again.

Steve took her by her shoulders and turned her towards himself. Her face was concerned and visibly upset. It was clear to him that something was wrong and that she was hiding it from him.

"Ornella, will you please let me know what is going on? What happened between two of you? Did you have a fight?" Steve showered Ornella with questions trying to understand the situation.

"Oh no—definitely not—don't worry about it."

"Ornella, I would really like to know what is going on. Please tell me. I see that you are very concerned and I need to know what is happening," Steve was trying everything to breakthrough her to find the information but this was just making Ornella more nervous and she felt she was going to explode internally from all of the pressure.

"Dad—please—don't ask me anything."

"So—You will be hiding this from me? What could it be so important that you decided not to share it with me, Ornella?"

"Alright, Dad—alright, I will tell you. Something terrible happened, really terrible."

"What do you mean terrible? Please calm down and tell me slowly everything," Steve tried to calm her down as she was becoming visibly upset.

"Dad—Igor had an accident at his work and he killed some man. He killed the wrong man who had nothing to do with the drugs, someone innocent."

"Oh dear God, that is terrible. Please calm down and tell me how is he, did you visit him and talked to him?"

"Yes, I went to see him but he's in a bad place. He's having trouble accepting what's happened. He is not himself anymore as if in shock. He's blaming himself and thinks what he's done cannot be forgiven. I don't know how to help him because he refuses any help. I am very worried and I don't know what to do now," explained Ornella.

"Oh god—this is not easy—but please do not worry too much. Everything will turn out for the best. I heard about many cases like this, unfortunately it does happen in his line of work but he will survive it, he just needs some time to process the information."

"I think in this case that time will heal his wounds. Igor looks like a strong young man with a strong character and integrity. I am convinced he will get over this in time, but you need to stay there with him and allow him time to get through this. Don't give up on him now." Steve was trying his best to provide an advice and to comfort his worried daughter.

"How will I do it, Dad, when even he doesn't believe in himself anymore. How will I continue believing in him?"

"Don't think like that now because you are under stress. You will be surprised how he will recover quickly."

"But I am very worried about him, Dad. I am very worried because what I see is so different from the man that I got to know. The disappointment on his face is too much to bear. It has been three days already and he is still exactly the same. He doesn't say much, I am worried about him and I cannot calm down because this really shook me up. I didn't expect this."

"No one expects anything like this. Simply this happens and that's the end. I don't want you to worry too much because he's strong like I said and I think he will be OK. He has to be OK, it's not like he has a choice.

"I stay behind my word that Igor is a young strong courageous man and with a lot of patience, things will work out in the end. Three days is not a long time, he will need many more days to process what's happened and accept his fate. Don't forget he's a trained police officer and he knew that there was always a possibility that things could go wrong when you carry weapons around with you."

A week has passed since the incident involving Igor and he finally was out. He came to see Ornella immediately.

"Igor, welcome to our home." Steve opened the door to Igor.

"We are very happy that you came to visit. Ornella will without the doubt be very happy indeed. Let me call her for you," said Rosie.

"Igor, please come in and sit down. How are you going?" asked Steve while Rosie is looking for Ornella.

"Yes, I am well, thank you. How is Ornella?" responded Igor changing the topic somewhat.

"She's doing fine, she is resting. She has to recover fully. You know what she went through and how difficult the situation was but I'm hopeful that that is all behind her and that she is strong going forward."

"Igor," yelled Ornella from the other side of the house. "I'm so happy to finally see you," she embraced him tightly and continued asking many questions. "How come you came here? Is everything OK?"

"Everything is OK," answered Igor. "I'm here because I want to talk to you."

"Let's go into the garden, it's nice day," suggested Ornella.

"Now what to say or how to start?" said Igor a little bit insecure and as if confused. He didn't look into her eyes, unnoticed she was following him around and trying to make eye contact that last longer than a second. Ornella started panicking as she noticed he was not himself.

"Please tell me what happened? I don't understand—"

"Ornella—"

"Yes—"

"You know I resigned from my position in the police. After what happened I couldn't continue."

"Why did you do that?" Ornella was surprised. She couldn't believe he rushed to make decisions like that after knowing how much he enjoyed working in the police and how he saw his career progressing through the ranks and lasting for many more years. She could not believe her ears and wished that perhaps he was just joking around. But no, he was not joking.

"I resigned. I can't work as a police officer anymore. That pleasure costed me too much. In the process, I lost my soul. You know I devoted everything to the police and that job. My work became my life but after what happened, I cannot continue. When I saw the wife of the man who I killed accidentally, everything was clear to me. She didn't say a word to me. She only looked at me but the way she looked at me, it was so sharp and so painful it felt like I was being lashed.

"Even now, I can see her angry eyes in front of me. These eyes are chasing me, I cannot find peace. I want to forget all of this but how, there is no way. I had to at least in one part free myself from the guilt by resigning from that profession and making sure that I will never do such a thing."

"Igor, I think you should not have done that. With time, you would manage to process everything and I know you would not forget it but for sure, you would push it away into your memory. I know that. I'm not imagining things. With time, the terrible pain does disappear and it gets exchanged with something different, something that still hurts but more quieter and weaker so we can stand it."

"No, no—Ornella—Please don't try to convince me. I made my decision and that's what I did and it's finished now. As you see we are different and we don't look at the world with the same eyes. I will live with this until the end of my life, this is my destiny."

"But Igor—what—what if you were in the war. How would you be able to survive those horrors?"

"I don't know; for me, this is worse than any war. You can't understand, it doesn't matter how much you try. It is hard I know because sometimes even I can't understand what's happening. I shouldn't have done that, but I did. Now, everything feels like it is finished for me.

"There are no innocents in this world, Ornella, we are all guilty of something. But everyone lives with their own guilt the way they can. I definitely made the decision to continue living with my guilt. That's why I resigned so this could not happen again. I would not have enough strength to survive this one more time. Even now, talking about it I feel I'm on the edge. Barely I got through this. Please believe me I couldn't do this again, I just couldn't."

"But Igor, maybe something like this would never happen again. You know what is the probability for this to repeat again maybe 1 to 1,000,000."

"I am not interested in that. I understand. I'm not crazy. I know all of that but I don't want to take any more risks."

"I think you are quite stressed and nervous about everything, I understand you, I think I completely understand you."

"I don't think you know, Ornella and I don't think you ever will truly know."

"What do you mean? What happened to you? Somehow you changed, like you are no longer mine, please be strong, you will survive this. I believe in you."

"Ornella—please—let's stop, I can't talk anymore—You are right I am nervous, I understand. It's not easy but I don't need you to feel sorry for me. I had enough of everything. Since the incident every single day that's all I'm listening to, other people feeling sorry for me and I can't take it anymore."

"I am not anyone, Igor. Will you put me together with all other people and anyway, I am not feeling sorry for you. I'm sorry if I made you upset, you know the best. I never had that intention. You must know that I am the last person in this world who wants to hurt you.

"Igor—I love you. First time in my life a man appeared and I was able to truly fall in love with you with all of my heart and soul. You know that, there's no need for me to explain. You are stressed and it's completely normal. I'm in a similar situation. I haven't been working and my career has gone nowhere. I think when I come back from Croatia I will focus again on my career but not now, I am just not capable to concentrate on work because of all of the stress."

"So—you will return back from Croatia?" asked Igor surprisingly. Ornella was left more surprised with his question.

"Well—of course—why wouldn't I return back?" asked Ornella still surprised with his question.

"Well—I don't know—I was just wondering," he said quickly and nervously looked around, everywhere but into her eyes.

"Igor, is there anything you are trying to tell me?" asked Ornella suspecting he was trying, to tell her something indirectly.

"Yes—you are right—I have to tell you something—"

"All right—you can say what you were planning to if it's that important."

She was not able to guess what he was trying to say but she did feel a cloud of negative energy wrapping around her and making her feel very uncomfortable. She felt pressure in every part of her body but her eyes were especially feeling the energy around.

Igor was observing her carefully. He was looking into her shiny beautiful hair, pale face red lips. As if he wanted to remember every part of her body forever.

"Igor, come on please, tell me, what is it?"

He suddenly pulled her towards himself and kissed her. But within seconds, he stopped and moved her away from himself.

"Ornella, I need to go."

"Where, Igor? Stay a little bit longer. What are you talking about?" she asked but her eyes were already filled with tears.

"I'm leaving today, I'm going to Brisbane. I came to say goodbye."

"To say goodbye!" screamed Ornella on top of her lungs. She was not able to move from the spot as she was frozen. She thought she was going to lose consciousness and fall onto the ground in any moment. He looked at her with eyes full of tears, understanding the heaviness of the moment.

"I am sorry—I have to go. I cannot continue living here anymore. Please don't cry. You will forget me, same like the nightmare you had."

"That nightmare I have never been able to forget. Why do you say that when you know I will never be able to forget you. Can't we go together? With you I will go to the end of the world," she said through tears.

"No, I'm not good for you. Something's broken inside and I feel really bad. I hope things will change when I leave this place when I leave this damn town. I don't have much strength. I'm leaving everything here. I don't have anything else and in some way, I'm glad for that."

"But you have me, Igor, you know you have me," said Ornella trying to convince him.

"Please don't, forget I belong to the past. I am not the best man for you. You need a different man, a more courageous man. Me, I'm nothing but a coward."

"I know the best, what is good for me and I know you are the best for me."

"You don't know anything. A day would come when you would also be disappointed in me. I wouldn't be able to stand that. That would actually finish me."

"You just believe in yourself, what you are talking about doesn't make sense. It really doesn't make any sense."

"Ornella…please, don't do this anymore," he begged. "Please, you know how much I love you. I love you too much to stay here. Forgive me if you can." With those words, he turned his back on her and walked down the garden path.

Ornella remained rooted to the spot, tears cascading down her face like rain. Her heart shattered into a million pieces, and she couldn't hold back her sobs. When she heard her own voice, she covered her face with her hands, feeling utterly lost and alone. She glanced up just in time to see Igor turn around and look at her. She could see the pain etched on his face, but it didn't stop him from getting into his car and driving off into the distance, leaving her behind.

In just ten minutes, her entire world had crumbled around her. Her eyes were still red and swollen, her face drenched in tears. She couldn't bring herself to turn around, to face the reality of the situation. How could he do this to her? He was supposed to be the one, the person she loved more than anything else in the world. What had happened to him? She was left alone with her thoughts, grappling with the pain and betrayal that had suddenly consumed her.

1000 questions were tearing her soul in pieces. She felt powerless and broken. She looked at the ring on her hand which he engaged her with. The ring was still shining with the same intensity as if it didn't know that all the love disappeared and there was no more reason for happiness. Everything around her was broken, all the lights were switched off and there was no more happiness. Not even a grain of it was left.

She had to survive all of this somehow, but it was not easy because she didn't expect this. Why did he do this and how does he dare? Questions, so many questions but no answers. Then she started walking towards the fence of the garden. She could not notice the beauty around her anymore, she was only looking in a direction from which Igor came.

With her long sleeves she wiped the tears looking into the distance. What else did she have? So much suffering and sadness in a very short time. First, getting sick and ending up in a hospital and now, she lost Igor. Other catastrophes she was able to survive but losing him that she could not. The love she was feeling for him was strong. How to tear that love out of her heart and how to continue going forward?

Inside her, spreading around like a storm was this great emptiness. Was this just some imagined situation caused by sudden changes or was this a new reality. This great emptiness inside her chest as if made of tin as if not a human anymore. The sky above her became grey, heavy clouds were accumulating as if a curtain on a stage.

The cold wind was blowing from the South. That same moment she thought she felt the smell of the sea and her eyes closed on its own. The wind was blowing and taking her tears into infinity. As the time was progressing, the wind was becoming stronger and stronger. Under wind's strength the branches of the nearby trees were bending. But not even that was able to move her from where she was standing. She wanted to attend the wind's performance which was prepared especially for her. Suddenly, the first drops of the rain brought by the wind from the distance was felt on the ground and in the air.

"My god—I am so desperate. How will I go on now—What do I do and how?"

Her hands again covered her face but this time, there were no tears left. As if the wind took away all of her tears. She was not sorry about that, may the tears go and go forever. The tears caused by deep pain, such a strange and uncomfortable feeling.

The drops of the rain started to hit the dry land bringing coldness. The cold was welcomed and she felt the rain on her face. Although she felt the cold entering her body and growing from moment to moment, she still could not move. Maybe she wanted the rain to fall on her and wash away all of her sorrows. Maybe that was not even possible anymore but she was desperate and expecting the impossible.

A wonderful man to whom she gave her love left her. How will she survive this now. His face was still in front of her eyes. She has lost the love of her life but why did this have to happen to her. The feeling of the loss was spreading around. How long will she be the one losing her loved ones.

"Oh God—Can you leave something for the others as well, do all negative and uncomfortable and painful experiences have to happen to me? What is the use of my youth, of my beauty, of everything, if you took from me forever the feeling of happiness? Why do I go on and what do I hope for?

"After everything that happened to me, I don't think that I have much strength felt. I feel so desperate. I think I have lost my faith and with it, hope. Without faith and hope, the man is way too poor and very tiny. As if I don't even exist anymore. Where is all that strength and hope that lifted me? Maybe died, or disappeared what could have happened to it?"

"Ornella, please get into the house. You will freeze out there in the rain," yelled Rosie. Ornella did not notice her nor did she hear her call. She was way too immersed into her own sadness. Rosie approached her and called again after realising that she did not hear her.

"Ornella, don't you see that it's raining, please come into the house. You will catch a cold in this weather. She is completely wet, Oh my God. Do you hear me?" asked Rosie realising that Ornella is not reacting and not responding.

Ornella turned around and with slow pace walked towards the house. The rain was falling heavily now. She looked up into the sky, feeling the rain on her face. The sky was still very heavy and grey. Was that God crying for her? Were these tears from her mother and her brothers? They were angels now, looking after her. Maybe, they felt sad for their loved one feeling such sadness, maybe they wanted to cry with her to reduce her pain that was now residing inside her. As if another dear person has died.

"My child, don't you see that you are completely wet. If I didn't come out, she would still be standing there," said Rosie trying to make a joke. Steve approached them.

"Was our girl crying?" asked Steve looking at Ornella. He noticed empty gaze and sorrow that was coming out of her eyes. Ornella did not respond, she had nothing to say. But they were her parents and her best friends, she will have to tell them. But now she was way too much exhausted and broken. Maybe another time when she finds enough strength, she will explain everything to them.

"Ornella, my darling. I asked you something, please tell me," asked Steve again but there was no answer coming from Ornella.

"I have to have a rest and change my clothes. I'm completely wet," said Ornella quickly when she noticed worry in his voice. She could not stand it. Her heart was broken in million pieces. She hugged him very tightly crying loudly.

"Don't cry, my only one, what's happened to you at once?" asked Steve but she could not stand it anymore. All of the suffering and pain went out from her. Steve realised that it is something serious and that he will not be able to stop her.

"OK, its OK, you can cry. All will be good. We all survived this in our youth and so will you. That's how life is. Somewhat cruel, sometimes sweet and that's how it is until the end. Just be strong and don't give up. You are my fighter, you are my only one. Keep crying, it is OK." Without her telling him what happened Steve realised on his own.

"How could he do this to me. I love him so much," said Ornella through tears.

"Please calm down, my daughter, everything will be OK."

"It will not be OK, how is everything going to be OK when he has left me forever."

"Give him time, he will come back, he will see. I am sure he loves you, you will see that I was right. You will be surprised when you see that he returned."

"Dad, don't try to comfort me please when you know it will not happen. First, he has gone to Brisbane. Everything is finished, it's completely finished. I'm not child anymore, you don't have to comfort me. I know that this is the end but I had such wonderful plans for us. Mum, please don't cry," she said to Rosie when noticing her crying next to them. They embraced each other in a long embrace.

"How can I not cry?" asked Rosie. "I am not made of stone. I am so sorry this happened to you, my darling. But why did this happen? I don't understand."

"Don't worry about it, Mum," said Ornella.

Chapter XI

A wide road in front of her as if an angry warrior full of revenge and rage. Her soul needed to rest and accumulate exactly enough strength which she needed for what she had to do next. There was one task in front of her that she needed to do. She had to travel to Croatia. Decision was made to travel alone. There was no doubt about it that she would go and nothing was going to stop her from travelling. All the fears and insecurities were gone now and nothing scared her anymore. Even a very small uncertainty and fear she felt initially were now gone.

In front of her there was an unknown future. Slowly but surely the last hope and faith will be returning back to her. She thought she lost them forever, but no, she only thought like that in the moment. When she thought everything was finished, it wasn't. The sky was clear from heavy clouds and the power of wind was back inside her body.

"No, I will never give up. I will not even think about that possibility. I will go back there. For so long I was not able to. I wish again to breathe in that air, to look at the proud mountains and blue sky. Maybe, I will come back with a different take on things, different feelings, maybe my life will have some sense again."

She wanted to be sure in her next steps. That was the main reason for going today into this interesting drive so that she could think about everything clearly. She has to be sure in all of her wishes, feelings, memories, ambitions and aspirations. The car stopped and she got out quickly.

In the sky there was a large bird. Ornella sent her a smile. She watched in awe the bird's magnificent performance in the sky. Its big wings were spread to the maximum and she was cutting through the sky as if the sharpest axe. How magnificent that large bird looked up in the limitless sky? The view completely took her attention, enjoying the birds' dance in the sky. The realisation came that she was not thinking about anything in that moment. Maybe that beautiful bird purposely arrived in time to improve her mood.

Ornella always loved planes, and like them she wished to fly off. Disappointment, that's what she was thinking about. That bird was like a metaphor for a huge plane which she will use to fly to her homeland.

"I am very happy, dear God, for letting me know who I was and where I come from. If only they were all alive so that I can go to them. Why did you have to take them away from me? Why did you leave me? What is my worth?" she was asking not knowing the reason.

As she was starting to feel worried, Igor's face would appear in front of her. She was still looking around and hoping that he would appear somehow in front of her. She was wishing to move on but moving on was not easy and she knew that she will need more time to get over him. But to forget him, that she will never be able to. He will forever live with her.

"Ehhh bird in the sky—If only you could tell him how much I love him and miss him. Maybe he would believe you. He did not believe me. Does he ever think about me, does he ever remember. I am sad because of him and confused, as if I have lost the most precious amulet which was keeping me away from evil. As if someone came and stole my happiness and now, I don't have it anymore. I'm just asking for how long will this emptiness live in me. I wish, as soon as possible to push this away into a memory so that I could go on my travels in peace."

Her wishes were pure and heartfelt but the passage of time was the only witness to their validity, and the ultimate judge of their fate. The threads that weave our destiny are often too intricate for us mere mortals to comprehend. Perhaps it is only through the trials and tribulations we endure that everything can ultimately fall into place. For what would be the purpose of shedding so many tears, if they did not hold within them some greater meaning? The ticking of the clock reminds us of the precious time we have, urging us forward to confront our old fears, while also igniting a flicker of hope that brighter days may lie ahead.

The love is always somewhere on the edge. Probably for that reason God created evil and hatred so that we are always in constant balance on this interesting but complicated planet. Must love be stronger from all of those evil powers, we cannot tell for sure because they are forever engaged in a battle and the winner is unknown.

Ornella was asking until when will the outcome of that fight remain unknown. She would even give her life in that battle of two powers if she would be sure that love would come out as a winner. If only old evil living in humans could disappear, even for a short time, it would be so good. No price would be too heavy to pay. But, such thoughts were useless when she could not change much around her.

Sadness again got it into her heart. There was too much sadness insight her to be able to easily get rid of it. Will things change for the better? Will this sadness disappear when she lands in her homeland? Maybe she will feel the happiness inside her, but the sadness will stay as well. Soon she will find out because soon she will travel there.

Suddenly she noticed the bird was no longer in the sky, she could not see her. Where did she go to and why? Maybe she will dance in front of another soul to turn their day into a better one. Ornella was grateful for moments shared with her. Still, she did not feel ready to return home. There was a need in her to still be there and think clearly what she was going to do and how and when and why. Her soul needed to understand the situation and reflect and process all things.

Her soul like a joyful squirrel from the forest was jumping around full of energy but her heart still wounded and heavy was pulling her down. How long will she be feeling like this? Like a bird in a cage. How long before she flies out of that cage? The steel bird will take her very soon towards almost forgotten memories to bring the past back to life.

In her mind she heard a strong scream when she saw her murdered mother on the green grass, warm from sun's light and red from her warm blood. Her fingers touched the ring in that moment. As if the feelings came alive and she completely let go walking around her past as if no walls remained.

The burden fell and she felt relief from being able to remember again and know where she was coming from. She remembered her parents, her brothers, their faces and their love towards her. As if a wave of nostalgia arrived and washed off her like a foreigner threatening to stay there forever uninvited.

The loss was felt in her heart. She was reliving the loss again. Her life as if on the edge of the cliff but she was able to find enough strength to fight with this and for the second time, she succeeded. In the corner of her wounded heart, she felt glad that it was like that, that she was able to survive it. When pessimism increase, a thought would cross her mind wishing for all of this to be finished as soon as possible.

Infinity of questions were circling inside her mind. How did that great love finish so quickly? It is true that life is made of small things, exactly those small things destroy big love. Everything turned against them and they could not survive. But why? Sometimes God is merciful. Sometimes his heart can tremble in front of a huge sorrow.

But does the heart of the executioner tremble after his victim's blood spills on his knife. Perhaps some ill fortune pushes him to do that. Maybe he does not want to but has to. Who knows what kind of agreements those damn souls sign in order to gain temporary fame and wealth? They do not know how short their glory will be and how long their eternal damnation would go for. Because their hands were dirtied with blood and their eyes blinded with lies, hatred and fraud.

Eyes full of hatred. Ornella remembered the eyes of the killer. Dirty uniform, dusty boots, bloody knife. She witnessed it all but now it was finished. It has ended. She wished it never happened. But the truth was difficult and clear. The memories returned back, flooding through the gate of her past. Was it a good thing her memory returned? Or did with its return her happiness left? It made sense, how could she be happy after everything she learned recently about herself, her life and her family.

The faraway land, her homeland was soaked in her loved ones blood and tears.

"May that land be damned. May all who walk on it be damned? Why were my loved ones treated like that, they were innocent and never harmed anyone?"

She collected her thoughts and got back into her car. It was still a wonderful autumn day. The wind was strong, blowing through the branches of the trees. The nature was calming down and getting ready for the winter. The golden leaves were everywhere as if informing all who were not aware that summer was long gone and winter was around the corner.

Ornella was packing her things and getting ready for her travel to Croatia. The flight was today and she needed to pack well. There was still enough strength and will in her.

"Ornella, please tell your father how are you feeling? Are you nervous? How is your health? You look a bit stressed to me," Steve showered her with questions.

"No—no—Dad—I am not stressed at all. Maybe a little bit excited but nothing to worry about, trust me."

"I think you made a decision to go very quickly, maybe we needed to wait a little bit more for more time to pass for you to feel better. You survived very difficult moments and I think travelling should have been postponed for some time. Please think one more time. I know you need to do this but maybe later, not now. Anyway, why are you in so much hurry?"

"Dad—Please don't convince me, the ticket is here and I am going today. Maybe you are right, maybe I did decide very quickly but I did decide and I am going. I don't know how long I will be there."

"So—where will you be staying?" asked her father Steve.

"I will stay in the town in the hotel. I will rent a car, I have to find an interpreter to come with me because I don't speak the language as you know."

"How do you think you will find your father?"

"Somehow, I will have to, even if I have to go to the end of the world. That's why I want to go as soon as possible. It's spring over there. Imagine the difference, here the nature is coming down and there it's just waking up. Maybe that is why I feel this energy. I want to go as soon as possible. I admit I didn't plan to go now but after everything that happened with Igor, I think it is for the best."

"I don't know, daughter, you are a grown-up person and you can decide about important things, but please listen sometimes to us old people. Maybe you should postpone this trip," Steve's still trying to convince her to stay. He had more reasons for that behaviour. He was thinking that her decision was made too fast and he was worried about her. He was scared he was going to lose her forever and he could not imagine his life without her.

"Oh—Daddy—" Ornella hugged him tightly. "You know you will never convince me to postpone this trip. But I know why you are doing this. I promise you don't have any reason for any stress. Everything will end up fine. I will stay there for some time and then I will come back."

"I admit, I am scared, you know what I'm thinking about."

"Dad, I will return back, don't worry too much. You know it's not good for your health. Anyway, I can't believe that you are worried about that. I was born there but I belong to this country now. Australia is my second mother. Here, I have lived the most wonderful days and it's thanks to you and Mum. How could you even doubt in me like that," said Ornella and hugged her father again.

"Eh—how not to worry, I have to worry because I love you so much. You don't even know how much you mean to us. You are our joy and happiness and without you we cannot go on."

"I understand that, I know it's not easy and I know how much you love me because I also love you so much. So very much, Dad. But everything that happened recently did affect me a lot and it's not easy to recover. I know that you understand me but don't be worried. In the end, everything will turn out for the best. I am sure everything will be OK. And anyway, where is that optimism that you were filling my head with all these years? You know, be positive, think positive, etc., etc."

Ornella tried convincing him and trying to reduce the stress in the room.

"You are right, my dear. I wish you have an excellent time there and if anything stressful happens, I need you to be strong and to face it with courage. I know not everything over there is going to be easy and you will need to survive some difficult times but like you said, maybe it's the best for you to go there and get a closure. Good luck, my little pigeon," Steve hugged her again tightly kissing her forehead.

***

Plane was already up in the air as if an eagle climbing up into the heights and no one was able to stop him. The large made of steel bird was cutting through the air and climbing up and up to the heavens towards the long-lost land. Not even in the wild dream could she imagine that she would be travelling to this land and not just any land but her homeland. The land that heard her first cry but she could not hear it because she now lived so far away. She was far away from her first mothers embrace. A destiny confused her roads and paths but slowly she will unravel them again.

The feeling inside her was complex and tense. Like rivers her lost memories were returning as if a grain of gold in the trough, it was hard to find them. She had to see through the fog into the crystal-clear memories and pictures. The times brought by wind were losing its direction, but Ornella was holding tight. The paths in mountain ranges were not easy to move through but she managed when she was there, although she so young.

"Why is my heart so heavy? Who is it crying for and why? I feel sadness for leaving. Australia is my mother; many years were spent there and I love this land. I never felt like an orphan, I always felt I belonged and that I was loved.

"My first pain was the memory of that tragic day. I think that memory will always live with me for all the years yet to come. Maybe with time, it will be weaker and paler, but I don't know. I accept it and can live with it because I know that is who I am and although they are so painful, those memories are mine."

Her thoughts were flying through the window whilst she was looking from the top on the cotton like clouds below the plane in the sky.

"Igor, you are still with me in my mind, although not here with me, I still feel your closeness, I still feel I am with you in your thoughts. How quickly did our story finish, before it really started. We felt connected from the first time we accidentally met and even now, although I know deep in my heart you have left me and gone from my life, in a way you are still with me. Maybe our paths will cross again in another life, maybe we will have more luck then.

"Who knows? It's not like we actually know what is going on around us. This life is sometimes just like a dream, pleasant and playful one night and a nightmare another. Deep down in my heart, I still feel your love and cannot imagine closeness of any other man but you. It is not logical and makes no sense but I'm not going to put a full stop on our love, not yet. I think you have already given up on me but I can't give up on you."

Chapter XII

Sun, stones and dry wind from the magnificent Velebit mountains in the Northern Dalmatia. Red barren land under the blue sky. Beautiful pictures of Croatian hinterlands, somehow warm and fragrant. Small, silted stones were breaking under Nikola's feet.

He stopped for a moment, in front of him a great vastness. Like an empire of various brawls and grey stones. Somewhere a gecko crosses his path and a well-known song of a blackbird is heard in his surroundings. Colourful work of nature around him but not one person coming into his direction or the opposite. Only sadness around him, great and indescribable sadness. Birds were flying around the sky joyfully and the nature was waking up in spring.

The sound of Nikola's heavy boots was echoing and disturbing the peace. It has been a very long time since he last walked through these paths. Different armies walked these parts and sowed their victims. Death was ruling this place and fear was still in the air. He remembered the peaceful times with nostalgia.

Now empty place, it looked like no one lived here anymore. Tears were falling down his wrinkled face. The strong spring sun was warming them and the wind sending them far into the land of his ancestors. In the distance you could clearly see the snowy peaks of the mountains. As if an unbroken chain or a shield of fallen warriors, long mountain ranges were spreading and coming together with the blue sky. Above the mountain ranges were white clouds, made of softest cotton as if only witnesses. With time, the wind would blow them away to bear witness to other unlucky ones.

From those bare mountains cold wind would blow in all seasons, it was a cold and dry wind reminding you never to relax and get used to the warmth of the sun. Nikola noticed the almond trees on his way. Pink and white dense flowers on the almond trees were spreading the sweet fragrance around and wind was pushing it far into the distance letting everyone know that spring was here and now.

This well-known fragrance woke in Nikola old memories and feelings. Some of the trees were already covered in green leaves but on the others, there was a lot of flowers still. The trees looked very old, bent under the burden of the times which passed them by over the years. Some branches were completely dry and showed no life left in them. There was no one there to cut the dry bits off and unburden the trees carrying dead and live branches. There were no people living here looking after their trees. Like the land, the trees were abandoned.

On his way he was passing by collapsed drystone fences. He recognised every detail surrounding him and, in that moment, he felt as if he never left this place as if the time never passed. His village was in front of him. He was able to see houses in ruins, burnt and destroyed after the war which finished in 1995 but still here in this remote village as if was only yesterday.

His steps became faster as he was approaching the village as if wanting to get to his birthplace in an instant. Nikola's house was at the end of the village; to get to it, he needed to walk through the whole village. Tears were falling down his face and he noticed his strength was reducing with every breath. Will he have enough strength left to make it? The thoughts were frightening him but he had to push through his fears and reach the target.

All around him were ruined houses of his neighbours, some had large bushes growing inside and around them. It was hard to recognise them. Nikola noticed an old house made of drystone and a woman sitting in front of the house. She looked very old and weak. Nikola looked at her, trying to recognise her and she also looked at him with her arms folded on her chest whilst sitting on a large stone. She was not moving but looking with intent to recognise him or maybe just surprised that anyone still comes to these forgotten lands. Nikola quickly wiped his face from tears as he was approaching the old woman.

"Where are you still coming from?" he was asking the tears. "All these years have you not been crying enough, have my eyes not cried enough? 100 times I thought I have no more tears to cry, my heart and my soul turned into a stone but you are still falling.

"Keep falling if that's what you want, let the wind take you through this wildland. This is the village I was born in. I went to that little school and had friends as good as brothers. If someone then told me that I will come one day to walk these paths through an abandoned village without any of my family left, I would tore his heart out with my bare hands. If I knew then what curse is waiting for me I would not believe it."

Nikola was walking and whispering to himself.

The village was quiet, extremely quiet and peaceful but then he was able to hear a dog barking. This suddenly woke him up as if he was walking and sleeping. He looked around to see where the barking is coming from. The small old woman in her black dress with the black head scarf was still observing Nikola with interest, trying to determine who was the foreigner coming into this village.

Nikola was looking around trying to determine if anyone else was living there but there was no sign of other life, only this old and lonely grandmother. A large german shepard dog run towards Nikola and he stopped. The dog stopped as well looking at Nikola with his big but sad eyes.

The dog looked at him as if not a dog but another human being, his eyes looked human, he stopped barking. Nikola knelt down and petted the dog. The dog responded with joy and happily wagged his tail As if it was a long time since anyone did something like that so the dog enjoyed the touch of attention. Nikola felt warmth around his heart seeing the animal so happy and welcoming.

The old woman approached them looking with interest at the face of this stranger who was playing with her dog.

"Is that you, Nikola, or my old eyes are playing tricks on me?" the old woman said and leaned forward towards Nikola to see him from closer to confirm if she was right.

Nikola stood up and looked at the old woman whose face was old and covered with wrinkly skin. Her eyes were deep inside her skull and the black headscarf covered her white/grey hair. Although it was years since he saw her last, he recognised her, she was his aunt Milica, wife of his distant relative uncle Ilija. She was in her late 80s at least if not more. Nikola was not expecting that she would still be alive and in the village at this time.

"Yes, it is me. And you, are you aunt Milica?" he asked to confirm if he was right as he could not believe himself anymore.

"My dear God, where are you coming from, my son, what stormy waters brought you into this abandoned and empty of people land?" she said while crossing herself in disbelief and shock.

"Apart from me and my old Ilija for many years no one lives here anymore," she added whilst clapping her hands still in surprise. At the side of the outside door of the old stone house an elderly man with the stick in his hand appeared.

"Grandmother, who are you talking with?" the old man asked looking curiously towards them.

"What trouble brought that mortal into this empty land? Here apart from us, there are only wolves and other wild animals. Humans don't live here anymore. Only graves are here and two of us still alive but approaching our death. What can we do when death does not want to take us still," the old man was talking but it looked like he was talking to himself more then with anybody else.

"Ilija, Nikola came back. Nikola returned," said aunt Milica to her husband Ilija.

"Whose Nikola, woman?" asked the old man surprisingly looking towards them trying to see.

"What do you mean who's Nikola? Dusan's son Nikola," she said quickly. Ilija came out towards them, slowly using his walking stick. His lower jaw was shaking from excitement and from old age.

"I can't see very well, grandma, he does look like Nikola. What if he is some kind of thief who came to hide in this rugged place?" suggested Ilija carefully still approaching them slowly.

"No Ilija, it's Nikola I recognised him immediately. He barely looks like himself. He turned into an old man himself," said Milica.

Nikola approached old Ilija and asked him, "Is that you, uncle Ilija? I didn't know you still live here," said Nikola now very close to Ilija.

"Well—I did not want to spill my blood all over the world, my hero. I said to my grandma, let everyone go but I will stay here. And, God is my witness, that's what happened, my nephew. Terrible armies attacked this place but with some luck they left us alive. Who knows maybe it would be better if they killed us then?

"We don't have a friend or a neighbour. We live here like in a desert, only us and wolves are left. So—tell me, my nephew—how did you get here? We heard you were killed, we thought all this time but look at you; you are alive and healthy," noticed Ilija.

"As you can see I did not die, uncle; the enemies arrested me and I spent all these years behind the bars serving the sentence. I survived for 15 years in the prison."

"You are very brave, my nephew, if you were able to stand such a long sentence. It is good you didn't die there. We heard the stories that our enemies were torturing our men in those prisons and that many lost their lives behind the bars. It looks, Nicola, you're very lucky because you survived that hell. Let's go into the house so you can get something to drink to give you some strength on your travels. We can sit down and talk a bit more. I am very glad to see you. I'm very happy that you returned back to your home village," suggested his uncle.

As soon as he entered the old house he was able to feel a well-known smell. He looked around the house and noticed on the stove there was a pot with boiled milk.

"Uncle, I see you have milk," noticed Nicola.

"Yes, I have one goat. We can barely look after her but we're still trying. We don't want to give up yet on this life, you know." Ilija was smiling and telling jokes, he was a joyful man, always around people near fire and song. There was no one in the village that knew more songs to sing.

"Tell me, uncle—where are your sons and daughters? Do you hear from them?" asked Nikola but at the same time feeling his heart becoming heavy. He remembered his family.

"My sons, they went to Serbia, far from their birthplace. My Nikola, I feel I don't have anyone, I forgot after all these years. I don't know honestly what I would like more, for them to stay here or to leave. It's not easy anywhere but that's our cruel life, maybe that is our destiny."

Nikola noticed on the wall there was a photo of St Nikola hanging on the wall. It was the saint protector which was celebrated by the family. He felt as if the saint is looking directly at him.

"Ilija, my uncle, what do you know about my family?" Nikola surprised him with this question.

Ilija looked at him with sorrow in his eyes. He was not talking, only looking at him. Then after a pause he started. "My nephew," started the old Ilija. "Don't you know anything?" he asked with fear in his voice. His old hands were shaking and his old eyes filled with tears. Nikola looked at him but then put his head in his hands trying to stop and not hear again the same story he had already heard.

"I know, uncle, I know everything, but still you tell me. I want to hear from you because I don't want to trust, Robert, damn him and all that is his. Oh God, what am I talking about? I have lost my mind."

"What can I tell you, my son, when you already know everything."

"I know, but I want to hear from you, please uncle, I want to hear—I have to hear it again."

"Nikola—that cruel day arrived, when they attacked, people run in the direction towards Bosnia. Your Vesna was probably not informed when other civilians were, I don't know. She probably wanted to reach the main road to connect with other refugees but she lost her way.

"She was found dead up north towards their lands. She probably knew there was a shortcut there and I think she was trying to reach the others. She was found by the soldiers from United Nations. They found her and your sons. They asked where to bury her and I showed them where the cemetery is and that's where they left them. What can I tell you, my son, what else can I tell you when you already know everything," it was getting harder for the old Ilija to speak.

Nikola was wiping tears from his face.

"Ilija, you have not told him everything," Milica interrupted them.

"What else, aunt? What else can you tell me?" asked curiously Nikola.

"Yes, there they buried them that is true, but I forgot to tell you that your daughter is not buried there. The woman that was with the soldiers told us that your Tina was alive but unfortunately from the trauma that she lost her mind. It was bad, my Nikola, listening to that story. I think they took her somewhere to hospital and who know what happened with the poor child. After the war, I heard from the neighbouring Croatian village that she died later in the hospital, but we don't know where she was buried."

"What are you talking about? My Tina, is this possible, maybe she is still alive."

Something in Nikola woke up and he stood up from the chair as if burned with fire.

***

The 4-wheel drive was skilfully fighting with the narrow and stony road. Ornella found way to face all the differences which awaited her in her birth country. It was true, everything was upside down in a sense but still she managed somehow. Her eyes were attracted to the place around her. It was very clear to her now why these scenes, stony grey mountains and distinct nature surrounding her were coming into her dreams. It all lived in her for all these years.

Excitement, happiness and feeling of drunkenness was spreading through her body. At times, she felt her heart will jump out of her chest. Such a wonderful feeling inside her. Magnificent moment. This old roads her destiny sacrificed her long ago for the lost ideals but now, the rivers of her life brought her back onto the old and well-known paths. She was brought into the embrace of her birth land.

The spring was waking sleepy life in this rugged place. In the distance, the snowy hills were shining in the April's sun, probably left from the winter. But yes, except of the magnificent nature and its beauty there was no visible human life.

"Ivana, are we close to the village?" asked Ornella the young woman curiously who was joining her on this quest. Ivana will be helping out with translation and locating the places Ornella wanted to visit.

"Yes—Definitely—we are almost there," answered Ivana.

Ornella wanted to notice every blade of grass, every bush. Her gaze was wandering around taking in as much as possible at that time. The energy inside her was alive and fast. This is how the dreams come true, she thought. This is how books are written, full of raw emotions. For a moment her thought wandered back to Australia, back to Igor.

"Oh Igor—how much I wish you were here with me to share this special moment. I know you would really like to see this place."

But he was not there next to her nor was he anymore in her life. He belonged to that part of her life which no longer was able to be made alive. But the moment in front of her was real and it was slowly coming true.

Suddenly, Ornella felt sadness and bitterness. The air around her was full of fragrance which leads only to one place in her past. She wished to again live through that enormous sadness which like a knife was tearing her soul apart. Her face was in line with her thoughts. Ivana, a young woman helping her to find this place was observing her with concern—

"Do you feel OK, Ornella?" asked Ivana.

"Yes, yes—I feel fine. Thank you, Ivana, there is no reason for any concern," Ornella was trying to convince her.

The thoughts as if released from prison did not have any borders. She wished to visit the crime scene, the place where her loved ones were murdered. She knew that was not the plan and that it was not a good idea but something inside her pushed her, something stronger than herself. She suggested to Ivana to go there but this startled the young woman.

"Ornella, that place is not easy to be found unless you know exactly where it is."

"Unfortunately, I don't know but it might be documented in the papers from the United Nations when they found me there."

"Maybe but I don't believe because they probably only put the distance in kilometres from the closest town or village," added Ivana.

"Still, I would like to check that. Maybe that place has a certain name. I only wish to be close to it and I understand it might be too hard to find it exactly."

"We would need to return back to Zadar to just speak with the government officials, of course if you want to. But I need to tell you this will slow us down a lot in trying to locate your father. I think you can always find that place later if you know what I mean," suggested Ivana.

"No, I want to return back to Zadar immediately. I am sorry Ivana but something is not letting me postpone this, something is pushing me towards that place," said Ornella while still looking through her window. No one was talking anymore only silence and spring all around them.

After more than an hour of driving in front of them was Zadar. An ancient Dalmatian town which stood the test of time and lasted for centuries. Various armies through the years conquered it but they were not able to take away its distinct beauty. And so, the centuries were passing and the rulers were exchanging, leaving its scars but still the beauty remained.

In some places, embraced by the Adriatic Sea giving it unique feel. Ornella thought how different from Australia, from the country where she grew up. This town was different from Spain as well, there was something quite unique about this place. Somehow in harmony with its past, present and future, this place was marching ahead.

"Ornella, let's get into this place, it is the United Nations High Commissioner for refugees. Maybe here they will be able to give us needed information. Anyway, I think it's worth a try. If in the worst case scenario, we don't find it here, they might tell us where else to look," explained Ivana and Ornella only nodded confirming her understanding.

After almost one hour of walking from one door to the next, she received a positive answer. On Ornella's face visible relief but also fear of seeing the place where the crime took place. It looked that she will be able to go there, now she was convinced, but if it was the best idea, she was not sure anymore. There was no return back. She will come face to face with her fear. She was not able to find the exact location but only a rough outline of where the place was. The good thing was that these regions in Croatia were not developing much, so they still look like they did centuries ago.

The car was travelling on the gravel road. Ornella was tense from enormous nervousness and not knowing what to expect. Even her breathing was slower whilst her eyes wide open were looking around trying to recognise anything familiar, but she could not. Then she asked herself quietly in her mind having seen the beauty around her, how did people here decide to fight.

But not everyone was thinking like her unfortunately. How many more children lost their parents in the wars and how many more will never have an opportunity to visit the graves of their loved ones. Thinking about this, she realised how she is one of the rare ones who was able to remember her past and her loved ones and now, she wishes to remember even the worst of her memories which she lived through as a 9-year-old girl.

Ivana stopped the car suddenly and showed with her hand that they were in the right spot. Ornella was still sitting in the car like frozen and was not able to recognise the place where they parked. Nothing looked similar to her memories and she still sat in the car. She felt that maybe all of this was not the best idea.

Still, she opened the door and got out. Fresh air smelt beautiful. She closed her eyes and smiled taking in the beautiful fragrance of spring. Now, the fear was gone and there was only feeling of freedom. She opened her eyes and started walking forwards.

A lot of bush and stones all around her. But where is that place where she lost her mother and brothers. She could not recognise it. She was not able to remember, maybe it was deleted from her memory. Ornella continued walking forward looking around to see anything familiar. Where is the huge old oak tree, her loved ones rested in its shade.

But when she realised that it was impossible, she knelt down on the ground and looked at the sky above her. It felt as if the earth spun in circles and she felt as if she was in the centre of the universe. There was only her and no one else there around.

"You—powerful heavens that write our destinies, you brought me back to these well-known pages of my life. Maybe I am not able to remember the exact place where I lost my loved ones, but I can remember this sorrow which embraced me from all sides. I remember the terror of that moment, the tears and my cry and the land beneath me soaked in blood. That blood was mine, coming from my wounded heart. The pain is still there and the wound never healed completely."

Cold sharp wind started blowing. Ornella got up from the ground looking towards Ivana who was waiting next to the car. Ivana realised it was the time to leave so she entered the car. Ornella, once more, turned around in a spin trying to suck in all the pictures around her. A gentle smile appeared on her face and she sent her sorrow into the distance.

The place where she was standing was special for her in many different ways. She continued towards the car and just as she was to open the door, she heard the children's laughter behind her. As if frozen in that moment, she stopped and turned again around looking in the direction of the laughter. Then she smiled in response to the laughter she heard, realising that it was her brothers' souls giving her the sign that they were well and not to worry.

"Let's go, Ivana, to my home village, it should not be too far from here I hope."

Several minutes later Ivana informed her that they arrived. She felt confusion and excitement. Looking around she wanted to remember every rock, every grass blade and every flower. The thoughts and memories returned into her heart and brought peace to her. Smile was on her face. She remembered that narrow path and her childhood games on it.

How was she able to remember all of this? How was she able to remember this path? Only now these narrow paths were empty. Houses in ruins, already old and overgrown with weeds everywhere all around. As they were driving through the village, she noticed a small house where smoke was coming from. This was where Ilija and Milica lived.

"Oh my dear God, I actually made it back to this long forgotten land. Ivana, please help me, I want to see who lives there, I want to ask about my dad."

Ilija and Milica heard the noise of the car and got out from their old house. They were indeed surprised when the saw two young women and a car.

"Good day, grandfather and grandmother, how are you?" asked Ivana politely.

"Thank you, my daughter, we are well, we are surviving somehow," said Milica but Ilija was not moving his eyes from Ornella's face. She looked known to him, but he could not remember.

"And you, my daughter, who are you?"Ilija asked directing the question to Ornella. But she did not understand so she looked toward Ivana to find out what he was saying.

"He is asking who are your parents?" explained Ivana.

"Oh—it is a foreign woman. I thought she was from here. She reminds me of someone, but I can't remember for the life of me."

Ivana translated what Ilija said. Ornella felt deep sorrow in her broken heart. She did not belong to these grey stones; she was a stranger in her homeland, but she wished so much that she was not. She could not change anything because she was a small pebble on the sand beach not able to understand the meaning but only able to understand that she knows nothing.

"Ivana, tell them who I am please," requested Ornella and Ivana told them. Their old faces reacted with surprise but their eyes still in disbelief.

"My dear and merciful god, I can see she is same as her mother Vesna, completely same as her. Her hair, face, eyes and the way she walks. Like an original copy. I was starting to get worried thinking am I seeing ghosts now in my old age. Tell her, my daughter, that her father was here today, he came straight from the prison and went to visit the graves of his loved ones. So many years nothing happens in this abandoned village and today two miracles. Glory be to God."

Ornella's heart was beating very fast now. That moment was here. Tension was in her whole body, but she felt it strongest in her head. She was going to visit the graves of her loved ones but she was feeling insecure and fearful. Her eyes were looking at her mother's wedding band. She came from a faraway land to return this special ring to her rightful owner. This wedding band belonged to her mother, it was always hers and Ornella was going to return it back today. Car stopped next to the graveyard.

Nikola was staying there as a shadow above their graves. Ivana felt nervous from this moment, but Ornella stepped out as a fearless warrior. From her eyes some strange fire was coming out, full of flames and revenge. The blood in her veins was boiling and the sorrow embracing her felt bigger than it ever was. That shadow over there, in front of her, he was her father. Her biological father. Ornella approached him very close. Her legs trembled from the moment, so she stopped suddenly.

"Cursed be every parent who buries his children. There is no greater punishment or curse from God as the death of your own child. If there was happiness, my children, you would be burying me on this graveyards and cry for me like this. If only we were lucky, my lambs. But our enemies cut your lives short and killed everyone I ever loved.

"What will your dad hope for now and to what God do I pray to and believe in? Ehhh God—Why you don't come and take me now and here so that I can stay with them forever," Nikola was praying looking down on their graves and then up towards the sky as if communicating with the God directly.

Ornella was looking at him feeling she could understand him. His body language was speaking instead of his lips and she was sure she knew what was going on. Nikola noticed that someone was near him. First, he thought it was the old uncle Ilija. He got up from the ground and stayed in awe looking at Ornella with his eyes wide opened.

Some huge excitement was awake inside her and she took off the wedding band from her finger and placed it on the grave. Nikola was looking all of this but was not believing his eyes. It was his Vesna, exactly same as that day when he saw her last so many years ago. He thought he had probably lost his mind and was seeing her ghost like in a hallucination but when he noticed the other young girl next to the car, he thought this was a reality and not a dream.

Without knowing anything about him, deep inside her heart she felt she knew him forever and was convinced he was a good man. "My father was not a killer, no, he was a gentle man who loved his family more than himself. He was a man who would jump alive into a burning fire if that would bring his loved ones back."

"Tata," said Ornella, looking into his eyes with fear.

Nikola was looking through the tears, his exhausted body turned towards her, facing her. He approached her closer, still looking directly into her eyes. Everything was clear to him.

"Tinaaaa—my Tina—is it you?" he asked from the top of his lungs. His long skinny arms extended towards her to embrace her.

A powerful strength entered his tired body and he realised his knees were shaking and the fear of the moment soaked in. Sadness and happiness in the same moment on the damp grass of his homeland. He hugged her with both arms, pulling her into an embrace which he dreamt of all these years. From the depth of his soul a roar released full of pain, loneliness and ill fate that one man can stand sentence to suffer into oblivion. In front of his eyes, the rays of sunshine and new hopes became alive after they were lost and abandoned years ago.

Their embraced bodies in that moment and quiet place where only the song of the birds disturbed the silence, time had perhaps stopped forever. That moment they shared lasted for eternity and it will never end. Two of them, different worlds and cultures but the same blood in their veins. The sound of their cry echoed from the distant hills and cold caves where their desires and unrest were hiding.

Under the sky of their homeland which gave birth to both of them, they were both standing. The only ones who survived and who were punished to suffer forever and to continue losing. In the distance, the sun was shining and showering the land with warmth and love.